# THE Rebel Princess

This damsel is NOT in distress!

# THE Rebel Princess

**This damsel is NOT in distress!**

# JANICE SPERRY

SWEETWATER
BOOKS

An Imprint of Cedar Fort, Inc.
Springville, Utah

This is a work of fiction. The characters, names, incidents, places, and dialogue are products of the author's imagination and are not to be construed as real. The opinions and views expressed herein belong solely to the author and do not necessarily represent the opinions or views of Cedar Fort, Inc. Permission for the use of sources, graphics, and photos is also solely the responsibility of the author.

ISBN 13: 978-1-4621-1430-6

Published by Sweetwater Books, an imprint of Cedar Fort, Inc., 2373 W. 700 S., Springville, UT 84663
Distributed by Cedar Fort, Inc., www.cedarfort.com

LIBRARY OF CONGRESS CATALOGING-IN-PUBLICATION DATA

Sperry, Janice, 1974- author.
  The rebel princess / Janice Sperry.
     pages cm
  Raven does not want to become a damsel in distress like her mother, but when Prince Charming shows up anyway--despite her lack of distress--and gets turned into a rat, Raven is swept into a magical adventure full of dragons, princesses, and evil Grandma Perilous.
  ISBN 978-1-4621-1430-6 (pbk.)
  [1. Magic--Fiction. 2. Good and evil--Fiction. 3. Adventure and adventurers--Fiction. 4. Characters in literature--Fiction.]  I. Title.
  PZ7.S7497Re 2014
  [Fic]--dc23
                                              2013050900

Cover design by Kristen Reeves
Cover design © 2014 by Lyle Mortimer
Typeset and edited by Melissa J. Caldwell

Printed in the United States of America

10  9  8  7  6  5  4  3  2  1

*For my family: Jason, Spencer, Alena, and Calton.*
*Thanks for the encouragement, support, and laughter.*

# One

I crept behind the black suit of armor and slid the diamond necklace inside its hollow leg. It landed on the growing pile of jewelry with a clink. A section of the wall behind me groaned and rolled forward, pushing me out from behind the armor.

"Stupid house," I whispered. "Why can't you ever be on my side?" The floor rumbled. Calling the house stupid probably wasn't a great idea. I scrambled for more solid ground and bumped the spiked mace leaning against the armor. It crashed onto the hardwood floor. *Oops.*

Mom ran out of the kitchen, the stench of burnt toast trailing behind her.

"What happened, Raven?" Her diamond-studded apron and matching tiara proved that it wasn't possible to sparkle and do useful stuff—like make edible food—at the same time.

"I thought I saw a speck of dirt on Dad's armor." I reached up to rub the breastplate with my thumb, carefully stepping in front of the mace that was now embedded in the floor.

"I heard a boom."

She would see the mace eventually, but I preferred to be gone when she did. "Maybe the house is adding a torture chamber?"

Mom put her hands on her hips. "Where's your necklace?"

I zipped my black leather coat up to my chin. "I'm too young for jewelry."

Her princess smile dimmed. "I always wore jewelry when I was your age."

True, but she was also locked in a tower with nothing but a rat for a friend. It's no wonder she eloped with the evil witch's son. "This is the real world, Mom. Seventh graders don't wear diamonds." And rats are not friends.

"At least stand up straight. A princess never slouches."

I continued to slouch. "I'm not a princess." The day my parents escaped from the Enchanted Forest was the happiest day of my life—and I hadn't even been born yet. I was not cut out to be a helpless princess.

My twin brother, Edgar, came out of the kitchen with a piece of Mom's burnt toast in his hand. Edgar got Dad's evil sorcerer genes. He gets to do magic and look ominous with his pale skin and black hair. I got Mom's adorable princess genes. I could go swimming in a mud pit and people would still ooh and aah over how cute I am. It's revolting.

Edgar waved his hand over the toast, and it went from black to brown. "We're out of butter," he said, holding his naked toast up for all to see.

He was the perfect distraction. "We're going to miss the bus!" I yelled, running for the door. Edgar shoved the toast in his mouth, snagged his backpack, and ran out behind me. Icy wind blasted my face and crept through the rips in my jeans.

We crunched through thick, old snow until we got across the street to the neighbor's freshly shoveled sidewalk, and then we ran to the bus stop. Our house was actually newer than most of the houses on the street, but it didn't look like it since Dad had built it with magic and surrounded it with a cloud of mystery. The outside was a dark, two-story building with creaky shutters. The inside changed from day to day, depending on the house's mood. We only allowed guests inside as far as the entryway so they wouldn't get lost when the walls wandered.

Edgar looked down the empty street and then checked the time on his phone. "Nice getaway. You could work on your timing, though. Dry toast isn't my favorite." He chewed on the remains of his toast and swallowed.

"Sorry. I panicked. Mom's jewelry is heavy. I could never escape a tower with all that sparkly crap around my neck," I said.

"We're in the real world, Raven. I think you're safe from towers."

"Mom still has jewels fall from her lips with every kind word and deed. Other fairy-tale magic could have followed Mom and Dad to the real world too." The jewel thing wasn't Mom's fault; it was her mother's. She had been nice to a fairy who "blessed" her to have jewels fall from her lips whenever she did something nice. It sounds great in principle but gets old pretty fast. Diamonds are a serious choking hazard. To top it off, the "blessing" is hereditary.

Edgar rubbed my head, messing up my hair. "Mom's jewels are not as horrible as what falls from your lips."

The "blessing" my grandmother received had two sides,

which her evil stepsister discovered after she ran off to meet the fairy and came back spewing frogs and slugs. What my evil aunt never knew was that the fairy used the same spell on her that she used on my grandmother. All the evil stepsister had to do was be nice to get rid of the frogs and slugs. Then again, maybe she did know and chose not to be nice, like me. My grandmother married some random king she met in the woods, and the evil stepsister escaped that fate.

What kind of king wanders through the woods looking for a wife?

I flipped my head, letting my hair fall back into place. "Ditching Mom's jewels isn't evil enough to bring on the frogs and slugs. I know my limits."

"Raven!" Mom yelled from our front door. She was a tiny sparkle of light in front of our dark house. "You forgot your necklace." She held up a necklace twice the size of the one I'd just ditched. The massive center diamond glittered in the morning sun. I could go blind if she ever got that thing around my neck.

I waved at Mom. "What did you say?" I yelled. Where was that bus? "Forget the tower," I muttered to Edgar. "I may need someone to rescue me from my own mother."

"Sorry, sis. I don't have a hero's bone in my body." Edgar leaned his useless body against an icy tree and grinned at me.

"You have crumbs all over your mouth," I said. Boys can be so disgusting.

Edgar brushed the crumbs away and then twitched his finger. "I just perfected a toothbrush spell." He smiled to show me his white teeth. Show-off.

The bus turned the corner and drowned out whatever Mom was yelling. I shoved Edgar out of the way and climbed onto the bus before she could cross the street and bring the necklace to me. The bus was empty, except for the driver, so I sat in the back and put my feet on the seat next to me. Edgar sat up front.

Amy got on the bus at the next stop. She was fairly new to the area and hadn't learned that I like to sit alone. Edgar stuck his foot out to trip her, but she stepped over him without even looking. He was getting too predictable.

"Raven!" Amy held her arms out and gave me a bone-crunching hug. "How was your weekend?"

"I had to inventory the dungeon." I learned long ago that it isn't necessary to come up with lies about my activities. No one believes me anyway.

Amy laughed. "You're so funny. Guess what I did?"

"Charm school?"

"No, silly. I volunteered at the animal shelter again. Those puppies are so gosh darn cute. You seriously have to come with me next weekend."

I think that if someone were to stomp on Amy's toes, she'd probably say, "Gosh darn, that hurt." Actually, I know that's what she'd say because I tried it once—accidentally, of course.

"Mm-hmm," I said as noncommittally as possible. What do people see in puppies anyway? They poop on the lawn and demand attention. You have to take them on walks every day. And what do they do for you? Lick your face. Gross.

The bus pulled over and kids pushed each other out of their way as they headed toward their preferred seats.

A boy smiled as he took the seat in front of me. "Hi, Raven."

"Hi, uh . . ." I searched my head for his name and got nothing.

"I'm Kevin Right," he said. "We've been in the same class since kindergarten. I'm in your Language Arts class."

The name wasn't familiar at all. "Of course, Kenneth. I knew it was you all along."

He sighed and turned back around.

"He's cute," Amy whispered.

"Boys are the enemy," I whispered back. I swore off boys the day Mom told me that one would rescue me if I ever got locked in a tower. I would rather spew slugs.

The bus pulled up next to the school, and the doors opened with a whoosh. Kids exited in an orderly manner since there were teachers outside watching. Edgar launched paper balls at them as they marched down the steps. I sat in the back and waited for them to clear.

"Take your time, missy," the bus driver said. "I don't have anywhere else to go today."

I tightened my shoelaces and walked down the aisle. Losing a shoe worked out for Cinderella, but it's not optimal for a seventh grader. Despite my efforts, my left shoe fell off on the last step, and I stepped in a pile of dirty slush before I noticed it was gone. I snatched the shoe before the bus driver could shut the door and drive away with it.

"What is it with you and shoes?" Amy asked. "You must have the tiniest feet ever."

I slid the annoying shoe on as I balanced on my other foot. "Do you know how hard it is to find shoes in my size that don't have a princess or an animal picture on them?" Mom's fairy godmother kept me well supplied with shoes, but I tended to lose them on stairs or any kind of incline. She says shoe loss is normal in fairy-tale-issued footwear. I think she should fire her shoemaker elf.

Edgar joined us as we stepped over a pile of blackened snow next to the sidewalk.

Amy checked her watch. Her locker was on the opposite side of the school from our first class, and she hated being late. "See you in class," she said. She ran up the salted steps and disappeared in the crowd of students filing through the shiny glass doors. Frost on the stone walls made the school sparkle like a castle in a fairy tale. I shivered. What a horrible thought.

"Why do you hang out with that little ray of sunshine?" Edgar asked.

Amy had appeared at the beginning of the term and always sat next to me. She never went away like the other girls, and I kind of got used to her.

"My slug and frog production came to a screeching halt when she showed up. I think her super happy aura cancels out my evil one," I told him. She also drives Edgar crazy. And he thinks she's cute—which drives him even crazier. It's a win-win.

We joined the crowd of students going through the front doors. The smell of wet shoes and school lunch eliminated any illusion of entering a fairy-tale castle. I would have taken a deep breath had it not been so gross.

We trudged through the crowded halls to our lockers. "Did you ever finish that poem you were working on last night?" Edgar asked.

I nodded. "We have to read our butterfly poems out loud today. Why does poetry always have to be about butterflies?" It was bad enough that my mother was named Butterfly. What kind of horrible parents name their kid after an insect?

"Would you prefer spiders?" Edgar ran his fingers up my arm.

I slapped his hand away. "Any subject would be better than butterflies," I said. I grabbed my books and trudged to class.

Edgar hadn't been forced to look at a line of poetry all year. He was lucky enough to get the teacher that made her students diagram sentences every day. His homework was color-coded and full of conjugated verbs. Mine was about flying worms.

A couple of girls walked past me, their heads so close together that their hair looked like one super highlighted mass of string. Their matching wedge sandals clicked in perfect synchronization on the shiny tiled floor. They'd probably been BFFs since kindergarten. That kind of friendship required an incredible amount of niceness, something I couldn't afford. Ever heard of an evil damsel in distress? I think not. I turned away from them and went into my Language Arts class.

There were plenty of good seats left. I headed for the one directly under the glaring eyes of a giant Jabberwocky poster, but Amy grabbed my arm and made me sit in the front. "I got us some great seats," she whispered.

"The great seats are in the back where I can gyre and gimble without getting caught," I said, pointing.

She giggled. "But you can't see as well from back there. And that poster is freaky."

Maybe a rat wouldn't make such a bad friend after all. At least they like hiding.

Mrs. Anders waved her arms to get our attention. "Quiet down, class. We need to get started so everyone will have the opportunity to share their butterfly poetry. Who wants to go first?"

Amy raised her hand. I sank down in my seat.

Mrs. Anders smiled so wide that I thought her face would crack. "Amy, you may go first."

Amy stood and cleared her throat. Someone in the back dropped a book, and the entire class laughed. Amy waited for the giggles to die down before she started reading. I stopped listening the moment she said, "Effervescent wings." After she finished, I clapped with the same lack of enthusiasm as the rest of the class.

"Who's next?" Mrs. Anders asked.

No one raised their hands.

"Miss Perilous?"

That is what happens when you sit on the front row. I stood and faced my classmates.

> Butterflies aren't so sweet.
> They taste their food with their feet.
> Butterflies are winged worms
> Covered up with dirt and germs.
> Should one splat on your windshield glass,
> It's just as gross as any bug you smash.

I sat down as my classmates clapped. Someone let out a shrill whistle, and a few others pounded on their desks. As a princess, I naturally attracted a fan base, even if they didn't know why.

I waved to my fans. More cheering meant less time for poems. I knew it, and they did too.

Amy shook her head.

"What?" I said. The last rhyme was a bit of a stretch, but it was all I could come up with last night between yawns.

"Mrs. Anders was looking for tranquility," Amy whispered.

"Then she shouldn't be teaching middle school," I whispered back.

The classroom door opened before anyone else had a chance to read their poem. Our vice principal, Ms. Darkwing, entered. "Mrs. Anders, I have a new student for your class."

Ms. Darkwing stepped aside to reveal the cutest boy I'd ever seen. His teeth even sparkled when he smiled. It was the first time I'd seen white teeth on a boy my age, except for Edgar, who cheated.

"Welcome to our class, young man. What is your name?"

"Eric Charming."

Every girl sighed, except for me. Charming? You've got to be kidding. A boy with the name of Charming only meant one thing—my fairy-tale roots had caught up to me.

My nemesis had arrived.

# Two

Eric Charming scanned the classroom. He totally ignored the Lewis Carroll shrine at the back and stared at Amy, confusion written all over his face. Amy was too sparkly for anyone first thing in the morning. Even Prince Charming was blinded by her cheer. He must have noticed how I oozed evilness because he locked his gaze on me next. We both narrowed our eyes.

Game on.

"Please take a seat, Mr. Charming," Mrs. Anders said. "There's an empty desk in the back."

Ms. Darkwing cleared her throat. "The new student should sit in the front so he can get extra help."

"I'll move back." I jumped up so the perfect seat in the back could be mine.

"Wait." The new boy held up his hand. "I'd like to sit next to Miss Perilous."

My jaw dropped open, and I plopped back down in my chair. He knew my name. I totally didn't see that one coming. Score one for Charming.

"You know each other?" Mrs. Anders asked.

I shook my head as he said, "I'm a friend of the family." And by friend, he obviously meant mortal enemy.

"I'll move back." Amy skipped to the back row and sat in front of the snarling Jabberwocky poster, leaving me alone with the cutest boy to ever walk through a classroom door. Some friend.

From close up, I could see a single freckle on the tip of his nose, slightly to the left. He wasn't perfect after all. I smiled and put my full attention on the crappy butterfly poem the boy from the bus was reading. I think his name was Kurt. Apparently no one told him that *fluttery* and *buttery* should not be put together in a poem just because they rhyme.

As my bad luck would have it, Charming was in my science and history classes too. I sat in the back. He never looked at me. I would have bored a hole through his silky brown hair if I had laser vision, but I didn't get laser vision. I got frogs and slugs. Mom's fairy godmother often suggested I do something nice so I could switch over to jewels, like pet a puppy, but we both know I'm a lost cause. She also knows how I feel about puppies.

"So how do you know Eric?" Amy set her lunch tray next to mine and flicked a lonely French fry off her chair before sitting next to me.

"Who?" I asked, pretending not to know what she was talking about. My stomach growled. I did not want the subject of boys to ruin my appetite.

"Eric Charming?"

"Oh, him." I nibbled my pizza and chewed slowly. I couldn't actually tell her our connection, not that I knew what that connection was. She'd think I was crazy, which would be fine if it didn't also include padded rooms and straightjackets. "I don't know him."

"But he knew your name."

"Only my last name. Maybe he's a stalker. He looks like the type." I probably should have listened when Mom ranted about her Prince Charming. All I remember is that he was really late. She waited seven years for him to rescue her from the tower before she gave up. He showed up after my dad helped her escape. I prefer to find something else to do when Mom and Dad recount their story because they get all dopey-eyed and giggly. Ew.

Edgar set his tray next to mine and stole my milk. "I hear there's a kid named Charming." He looked at me with concern. Bless his cold little heart.

I nodded and dropped my voice so Amy couldn't hear. "We've met."

He leaned closer and whispered, "I could turn him into a toad."

I shook my head. "Then someone would expect me to kiss him."

Edgar choked on my milk. Served him right. I grabbed his unopened milk carton and let him keep mine.

"Hi, Edgar." Amy looked around me and smiled at Edgar.

"Amy." Edgar shoved half a piece of pizza in his mouth and got a little sauce on his chin. I didn't tell him about it.

One of the cheerleaders—they all dressed alike and wore their hair the same way, so I couldn't tell which one it was—came over from a nearby table. "Hi, Edgar." She giggled, which is what cheerleaders do around Edgar. I'm not entirely sure why.

Edgar nodded at her. His face was clean. I'd forgotten about his self-cleaning spell. Drat.

She turned to me. "Raven, your hair looks adorable.

I don't know how you manage to always look so cute. Maybe it just runs in your family." She gave Edgar a nauseating smile before rushing back to her table. They all leaned together and whispered while casting furtive glances our way.

"I wonder what they're all talking about," Amy said.

"How breezy it is between their ears?" I guessed. The cheerleader had just called me cute and adorable in one breath. I'd never been so insulted.

Charming came into the cafeteria surrounded by a gaggle of girls. He headed straight for the salad bar. Salad? What kind of sicko was I dealing with? He even took some spinach.

Our eyes locked for a moment. Then his gaze flickered to Edgar. His jaw dropped open. I smiled. *That's right, Charming. There are two of us. You'll have to go through my brother before you can get to me.*

"I'm done." Edgar stood, grabbed his tray, and left. We really needed to work on that whole twins-reading-each-other's-minds thing.

"I got some new nail polish." Amy sipped her milk. "It's pink and glittery. What are you doing after school?"

My fingernails will never be pink or glittery. "I'm going rock climbing."

"Really?" Amy studied her nails. They twinkled in the cafeteria lights. She bit her lip for a second and then blurted, "Could I come?"

I almost snorted milk through my nose. "You want to go rock climbing with me?" I'd been rock climbing for a few years, trying to prepare myself for a tower escape, but I'd always gone alone.

She nodded, her red curls bobbing all over her head.

"Sure. First we go rock climbing, and then we go to my house and do each other's nails. I have black polish too, if you prefer." For some reason, she wouldn't look me in the eye.

The giggles coming from the cheerleader table somehow made a tiny spot in my chest feel hollow. Rock climbing with someone wasn't the same as being nice to them, and Mom would be horrified if I came home with black polish. "Let's do it."

It was her turn to be surprised. "Really?"

I nodded. "Black nails could be cool. Are you sure about rock climbing? It's a challenging course."

"I don't have a problem with heights. Climbing is easy. I do it . . . often."

We put our trays away, staying clear of Charming and his groupies. I almost felt sorry for him. Almost.

"I wish we had more classes together," Amy said.

We had six out of seven classes together because I had skipped seventh-grade math and went straight to eighth-grade honors. Mom says it's because I'm too calculating. Dad says it's because I inherited his evil genius, which might be true since Edgar is in that class too. "You don't want to be in my math class."

"You're right. Math isn't my best subject. I like the arts."

The bell rang. I hurried to my locker and stood on my toes to yank the math book out from under the stack. My history book slid off the pile, and I caught it with my face. I used my one free hand to stop the rest from crashing into my head. Stupid petite princess genes.

A freakishly tall boy came up behind me and pushed the books back into my locker before they could smash my nose. It was Charming.

"Thanks," I said, slamming my locker shut and avoiding eye contact. One look in those eyes, and I could be doomed. Mom once spit out an emerald the same color as his eyes. Okay, so I looked for a second, but only long enough to verify that he was still the enemy. I could never put my life in the hands of a boy. Who knows when those hands were last washed?

"We may be on opposing sides, but I won't stand by while an evil witch gets beat up by her own textbooks." His eyes were also the same color as a frog I once spewed.

The only thing I could say to him would produce more frogs, so I turned my back to him and went to math. I sat next to Edgar in the back row. "Charming just called me an evil witch."

Edgar tapped his pencil against his chin. "Is he sucking up to you or something?"

"I don't think so. He said it like it was a bad thing."

"Technically, it is."

I stared at him. How could he say such a thing?

Edgar twitched his finger, and a small flame appeared in his hand. I didn't talk to him for the rest of the class. It wasn't fair that he got to play with fire and I was stuck avoiding Prince Charming.

My next class was CTE, which stands for Currently Torturing Equally, or something like that. It's what used to be known as Home Ec before it became a requirement for every student in seventh grade.

The chair next to my assigned seat was empty. Weeks of strategically losing my sewing needles on the seat next to me had finally paid off. I was alone at last. Amy waved at me from the other side of the room. I waved back, trying to ignore that strange, hollow feeling in my chest. It couldn't be guilt. The needles weren't *that* painful.

The teacher came in with Charming. "We have a new student. This is Eric Charming." Mrs. Cutter pointed at the empty chair next to me. "Sit next to Raven. Raven, stand up so he knows who you are."

I folded my arms. A Perilous does not stand for the enemy. Charming sat and scooted his chair as far away from me as it would go, which was fine with me. I was out of needles.

"We are heading into the sewing lab so you can finish your bags. Anyone have a question?"

Charming raised his hand.

"Ah, yes, Eric will need some help getting started. Raven, please take him to the supply closet and help him get his supplies."

Me in a closet with Charming? Ew. "I don't think I can reach the thread. Maybe someone taller should help him."

"Then find someone else to help you," Mrs. Cutter said, which really meant, *I am not getting paid enough for this.*

Every girl in the class raised her hand, except for Amy. She was studying her sparkly fingernails.

"Amy can help," I said. She shot me a bewildered look. I almost felt bad, but then I settled for confused. I'd have to ask her about it later.

Amy and I trudged across the hall with Charming close behind. I opened the door and tapped the light switch. The room was full of sharp stuff, ugly buttons, and half-thought-out craft projects. I pointed to a box full of cloth. "You'll need some of that." When no one was looking, I grabbed a box of straight pins for future use.

Amy lifted a container from a shelf way over my head.

"You'll need a spool and also a bobbin. The scissors are in the sewing lab."

The door clicked shut. Amy and I both jumped. She held the thread box out to Charming. "Once you find the cloth you want, you'll need some matching thread."

Charming looked back and forth between the two of us. He ran his hand through his thick hair. "Okay, I give up."

"We don't take prisoners." I faked a laugh. What was he talking about? Amy was a regular person who was going to think he'd fallen off his rocker if he started talking fairy tale.

Charming turned the light off. Amy glowed in the dark. Regular people don't usually do that.

"Amy, why are you still sparkly?"

Amy turned the light back on. "I'm studying to be a fairy godmother. The magic makes me light up." Once again she wouldn't look me in the eye.

She was odd, but I never considered that she might be magical. Come to think of it, though, no one else sparkled quite as much as Amy.

"But Edgar is magical. He's not sparkly," I said.

"He's a sorcerer," Amy said. "Sorcerers aren't glittery like fairy godmothers."

Charming snorted. He seriously needed to work on his charm. "You didn't know your best friend wasn't from the real world? Typical Perilous. Always focused on yourself. I knew the moment I saw her this morning. She's oozing magic." He turned to Amy. "What are you doing with an evil witch?" He shifted to a heroic pose and raised his eyebrows. "Are you going dark?"

Amy stood up straight, and red sparks shot from her

ears. I'd never seen her like that. It was awesome. "I am not going dark. I'm working on earning my wings. I came for the extra practice."

Her speech sounded rehearsed, which was not awesome. I wasn't sure what to think about Charming accusing her of being my best friend either. She couldn't really be my best friend because BFFs wear matching shoes and tell each other everything—at least, that's what I've heard. I had no idea who she was. That had to count for something. She did wear cute black flats, though. I wouldn't mind a pair, only smaller and not as sparkly.

"Extra practice?" Charming said.

"Princesses attract trouble. They are always in need of a spell or two." Amy's face was a brilliant red.

"You're taking advantage of an innocent princess?" Charming said. "What if she needed help and no one came because they thought a real fairy godmother was already on the case?"

"She's not exactly innocent," Amy sputtered. "And she isn't helpless either."

"I'll have to report you as soon as I can return to the Enchanted Forest. There must be some kind of fairy godmother council or something." He turned to me. "What have you done with Princess Butterfly?"

How behind the times was he? No one called Mom a princess anymore. She handed out healthy treats at the school carnival every year. Most kids avoided her out of principle, including me.

"I left her at home to do whatever it is she does all day. And we can all be sure that it isn't making cookies." I reached into the cloth bin and grabbed a piece of cloth, which just happened to be a little pink number covered in lacy hearts. I shoved the cloth in his hand. "Mrs. Cutter is going to freak if we take any longer."

He shook the pink cloth in my face. "We aren't finished. We will talk again," he said. Then he stormed out of the room.

Amy picked a spool of pink thread and a matching bobbin from her box. "I don't like him."

"That makes two of us." I looked up at her. She'd been lying to me from the moment we met, which meant she had to be evil. I could understand the need to keep her identity secret. That's something you only reveal to your BFF. Maybe we could be evil together. Not exactly BFFs, but close enough to wear matching shoes, if I could find some in my size. "What spells have you been practicing?"

"The first spell I perfected was the cancellation of your frogs and slugs. It only works for a few hours, so I've gotten pretty good at it." She shuddered. "I don't like slimy things."

"You could have told me sooner." We closed the closet door behind us and took our time walking back to class. "I've been nice to people all this time, and I didn't even have to be."

"I wasn't sure how you felt about the whole fairy tale thing."

"Mom's fairy godmother still visits now and then. She's my main source of shoes."

"I thought your shoes looked fairy-tale made. You aren't mad, are you?"

"Nah. I don't miss the frogs and slugs at all."

We walked across the classroom, and Amy put the thread and bobbin on Charming's table. He grunted.

"Oh, are you making a bag for your little sister?" Mrs.

Cutter asked him. She fingered the pretty pink fabric I'd picked out.

Charming shook his head. "I don't have a little sister. Why?"

"Well, um. It's okay if you prefer pink."

Charming looked at the material, and his face turned a matching shade. "This is what Raven gave to me."

"Raven." Mrs. Cutter turned to glare at me.

"The closet was dark," I said, keeping my face straight.

Giggles erupted around the classroom.

"Why does the new guy get all the luck?" a boy asked.

"Take Eric back to the closet and help him find something more to his liking."

"I'll do it!" several girls said at the same time.

"I volunteer," another said.

"It's okay." Charming stood up. "I know my way to the closet. I don't need help." He snatched the pink cloth from the table and left without looking at me.

# Three

The climbing gym was almost empty when Amy and I arrived. That was how I liked it. We left footprints on the padded floor as we passed by fake rock walls covered in colorful handholds. I removed my shoes, because losing a shoe on the climbing wall was awkward.

"What are these ropes for?" Amy asked.

"Safety. In case we fall."

"Oh. I've never been to a place like this before."

We buckled our harnesses and clipped onto the most advanced climbing wall. There was a mysterious door at the top I wanted to go through. Rumor had it there were free drinks and chocolate bars up there. I usually made it halfway before I lost my grip on the tiny handholds and had to rappel back down.

"Are you sure you can start with this one?" I pinched Amy's thin, chicken arms. "It's pretty hard."

"It's not too different from the cliffs back home." She took hold of the wall and scrambled up like she was running across a field of daisies. She swung her legs over the roof and looked back down at me. "Where does this door go?"

"I've never been up there," I said through my teeth. She did say she climbed often. I just didn't believe her.

She vanished from the ledge, and the door clicked open and shut.

I breathed in the sweaty smell that was the gym and focused on the wall. This time I was going to make it. There was no way I was going to let Amy outshine me. It wouldn't be so hard if they hadn't built it with giants in mind. The smaller handholds were the right size; they were just too far apart, and the wall wasn't completely vertical. It curved out so the climber had to hold on to the wall rather than stand on the footholds. I grabbed hold of the wall and started my ascent. Someone clipped in next to me and easily matched my pace.

"You know, most evil witches use the stairs." Charming grinned at me.

My hand slipped. I dug in my toes and held on with my other hand. "That is why I am learning how to climb walls," I said through my teeth. "They don't give stair access to princesses."

"You?" he scoffed, "A princess? Next you're going to claim you aren't a Perilous. I knew who you were the moment I saw you. You all have that same evil glint in your eye."

"Thank you." I found a good handhold and pulled myself up the wall. "I have never pretended not to be a Perilous."

"Are you his little sister?"

"I was born first."

"Not your evil twin. I mean Darkly."

"My dad changed his name to Harold after they escaped the Enchanted Forest. Darkly is a pretty weird name, even for a Perilous." Why did Edgar always get to be the evil twin? It wasn't fair. And why was Charming so interested in my parents?

Charming paused, and I took the handhold he was reaching for. "Darkly isn't old enough to be your father."

"That's what he always says. To be fair, my parents don't act old enough to be parents, but I think that's because of how they were raised. My mom didn't get much of a childhood, being locked up in a tower for so long. My dad's mom was an evil witch and wasn't the nurturing type."

Chatting helped me keep my mind off climbing. I passed the highest point I'd ever reached without really noticing.

Charming's hand slipped off the wall, but he caught himself. "Your mother is Butterfly?" His face was pale.

"Yep. Can you believe she didn't change her name when she got the chance?" I reached up and touched the roof. A little thrill ran through my veins. The roof stuck out over the wall and was an extra challenge at the end of the climb. I had no idea how to maneuver around and over it, but I was there. I grabbed a handhold. I could do this.

"But Butterfly is only seventeen years old."

I studied the wall. "She was seventeen when she left the Enchanted Forest. That was fourteen years ago."

"Fourteen years ago?" He swung his freakishly long legs over the roof and reached a hand down to me. I ignored it.

"Give or take a few months. Could you scoot to the left? I might kick you on my way up."

"Butterfly and Darkly eloped a few days ago."

"Nope." I grabbed a handhold, and my fingers slipped. Charming grabbed my arm and hauled me over the roof. "I don't need your help!" I yelled.

"I could put you back."

My arms felt like rubber, and the ledge looked really hard from here. "I'll do it next time."

"Fine." He ran his fingers through his thick hair. Could his hair possibly be as soft as it looked? It probably smelled nice too. I snapped out of it in time to notice that he wasn't standing in front of me anymore, and the door was open. At long last, I went through the door I'd been climbing toward for almost a year. True, I didn't make that last bit by myself, but I would have if Prince Charming hadn't been so obsessed with rescuing damsels who were not in distress.

There was nothing in the room but a dusty couch and dark corners. No drinks. No chocolate. "I spent all that time working my way up that stupid advanced wall for this?"

Then I noticed Charming sitting next to Amy on the couch cupping his head in his hands. "The room isn't that bad," I said.

Amy scooted away from him and patted the synthetic green leather next to her. "There's room."

"The layer of dust on that thing is as thick as my dad's armor." Also, Charming didn't look well. He could be contagious.

"What's with him?" Amy pointed her thumb at Charming.

"I don't know. Well, I'm done climbing. Let's rappel down and go do our nails." Rappelling is much more important than climbing. Princesses usually have to get out of towers, not in.

"Fourteen years," Charming said.

"What?" Amy asked.

I shook my head at her and put my finger over my mouth. Charming was the last person I wanted to have a conversation with. She didn't look at me.

Charming sat up, smearing dust all over the back of his shirt. "Where have I been for the last fourteen years?"

I checked the clock on my phone. There was precious little time left before I had to be home for the disaster that Mom calls dinner. This was hardly the time for Charming to go through a life crisis. "You're only thirteen, Charming. It doesn't take an honors math student to figure out the flaw in your question."

"No. You don't understand. I'm the Prince Charming assigned to Princess Butterfly."

My jaw actually dropped open. I snapped it shut. "How is that possible? Mom's Prince Charming was with them in the Enchanted Forest fourteen years ago. You weren't even born then."

"I was eight when the magic calling came. There wasn't any other qualified hero. I didn't want to go because the princess was so much older than me. My mother told me it was all right to prepare for a few years and then true love would conquer all, even our age difference. I practiced with my sword and prepared to fight the witch. I couldn't call myself Prince Charming if I didn't believe in the power of love." His lip trembled for a second. Then his eyes went hard. "I admit I put off saving your mother for as long as I could. By the time I found her, she had already escaped and was running off to the real world with your father. Then your father stole my sword and cursed me to follow after them. I can't return to the Enchanted Forest until I find my true love. But I don't want true love. I want my sword back."

"Harsh," Amy said.

Charming thumped the couch with his fist, sending a massive dust cloud into the air. "I just can't figure out how I disappeared for fourteen years."

"It depends on how the curse was worded." Amy pulled a sparkly pencil out of her back pocket. The back end of the pencil curved into a heart. It was revoltingly cute. "Watch this." She cleared her throat.

> *Couches green*
> *Are so obscene.*
> *Couches blue*
> *Are strong and true.*

She waved her arm in a big circle until sparkles appeared in the middle of the heart. The couch shuddered and turned orange.

"I don't think the couch likes to be rhymed with." I sniffed. It smelled like dusty oranges.

Amy tapped her pencil against her leg. Red sparks fell like sand from the end. "I'm still learning."

I turned my attention back to the problem at hand. "Are you saying my dad messed up his curse?" I asked her. "He's a great sorcerer."

"He is now, but your dad came up with that curse when he was only seventeen," Amy said. "Whatever he said must have sent Charming fourteen years into the future."

"I don't remember him saying anything about cursing Charming, but I never really listen to him anyway." I checked the clock on my phone. We needed to hurry. The gym was going to close soon. "I guess you'll just have to grow up and find your true love before you can go home. Your parents probably already think you're dead, so it won't make any difference after all these years."

"You aren't helping." Charming pulled his knees up to his chin and rested his forehead on them.

"The important thing is that we all made it up to the

mysterious room," Amy said. She patted the orange couch and looked around. An old-fashioned lightbulb hanging from a chain flickered. "Yay."

"Not the way we planned," I grumbled.

"Raven would have fallen if I hadn't grabbed her," Charming told his knees. As if dragging me off the wall fixed anything.

"I was strapped in. There was no danger."

Amy clapped her hands and little sparks erupted around her. "What? He saved you? You have to kiss him, and you can live happily . . ."

I put my hand over her mouth before she could finish. "I would rather kiss a rat."

Something rustled in a distant, dark corner, and the air filled with a swampy fog. Blue sparks swirled around us, picking up speed and blurring in the murky air. When the fog cleared, Prince Charming was gone, and in his place sat a white rat.

"I take it back," I said. "I would rather not kiss a rat. Ew."

# Four

"What did you do?" Amy stared at me, her eyes wide.

"Me?" This mess was not my fault. Charming's whiskered nose twitched, and he emitted a strange, squeaky sound. Angry rats are not nearly as cute as happy rats, not that rats are ever cute. I scooted away from him. "I didn't do this. I can't do magic. I'm a princess, remember? You're the one with a wand."

Amy used her sparkly pencil wand to scratch her head. She waved it around, and I ducked. "Relax, I'm not doing magic. I'm thinking."

Good thing. I saw what she did to the couch. No way did I want to be in the line of fire next time she tried a new spell. I totally lucked out with her cancellation of my frog and slug spell.

"You're a princess."

I buried my head in my hands. This was going to take a while.

"You had your shot to thank him for saving you with a kiss, but you rejected him." She scrunched her eyebrows together in concentration.

"He didn't save me. I was tethered to the wall. The worst that could have happened is I wouldn't have made it up to this room." I ran my finger along the dusty couch. "It's hardly worth a kiss."

Charming's whiskers twitched again. He had a little brown spot on his nose where his freckle had been. I wasn't sure if he was agreeing or disagreeing with me, not that it mattered.

"But you'll have to kiss him now," Amy said. "Otherwise, he'll remain a rat."

"Maybe he likes being a rat." My lips touch lips that had touched spinach? Ew. "I can't just kiss him without knowing how he feels about it."

Charming scurried off the couch and hid behind it.

"See," I said, pointing to his hairless tail sticking out from behind the couch. "He doesn't want to kiss me either. You're learning about magic. You fix him."

Charming's tail vanished behind the couch.

"Raven!" The gym manager yelled from below.

I left Amy with the rat and went to see what the guy wanted. "What?"

He stood below me with his coat on. No one else was in the building.

"Good job getting up to the room. I would have cleaned it up if I knew you were going to make it all the way this time."

"The dust is pretty thick, sir. You might want to clean it up anyway." And put a table full of chocolate bars in it.

He rubbed his protruding stomach. "Sure. I'm locking up, kiddo. Fly on down, and bring your friends with you."

"Okay." What else could I say? I hurried back into the

little room. "Amy, we have to do something. The gym is closing, and he knows there are three of us up here. We can't go back down with a rat and no Charming."

Amy took a deep breath. "Okay, Charming, I'll do a temporary spell to make you look human again."

One pink eye appeared behind the couch.

"Although, I should warn you that I haven't had any formal training, but I've read some great books." The eye disappeared. She took a deep breath. "Raven. Move the couch."

I pulled the couch away from the wall. Charming had his pink little tail wrapped around his head.

Amy tapped her chin with her wand and cleared her throat.

> *Kissing a rat is not a joy.*
> *You need to be a princely boy.*
> *Some frog, some snail,*
> *And absolutely no naked rat tails.*

It was better than her butterfly poem, which didn't say a lot. Charming's legs stretched, and his head swelled. When it stopped, he looked more like himself, only with a layer of white fur and a pointier nose.

He examined his arms. "Why am I still furry?"

"I did say it was a temporary fix. Raven, you can kiss him now. He's more boy than rat."

I tightened my ponytail. "Let's figure it out somewhere else. They're locking up."

"I knew you were an evil witch," Charming said. He brushed past us and went out the door that was no longer so mysterious and exciting. Amy and I followed him down the wall.

"I'm not sure what went wrong," Amy said. "The rhymes were so lovely."

Charming stormed, or rather angrily scurried, through the front doors. We paused so I could slip my shoes on and then ran to catch up. He was freakishly fast.

"You think I did that?" I yelled at the back of his head.

He stepped over a pile of dirty slush and crossed the street.

"I can't do magic, crazy boy, but my father can. I'm sure he doesn't hate you now. He could help."

"You can stop yelling, Raven. He can't hear you anymore," Amy said, coming to my side. "And I doubt he would want to ask the person who cursed him and ruined his entire life for help."

She was right. Yelling didn't do any good at all, and it's not like I cared. He was Prince Charming, the enemy. It was in my better interest to let him be a rat. I tightened my ponytail again. "What is up with my hair? It never comes loose." I checked the clock on my phone. "It's late."

"I didn't expect climbing to take so long either. We'll do our nails another day, okay?" She didn't look as disappointed as I thought she would.

"Where do you live anyway?" She couldn't live far, since she rode the bus with me. The idea of having black fingernails had grown on me.

"In the woods behind your house."

"You live where?" No one goes in the woods, let alone lives there, except for the beast. No one has seen it, at least no one who lived to tell the tale, but you can hear it howl when the moon is full.

She grinned, tapped herself on the head with her wand, and vanished.

A car that might have once been green pulled to the side of the road. The passenger side opened with a screech, and the boy from the bus got out.

"Hey, Raven. What are you doing out here by yourself? Do you need a ride?"

I noticed a mom-aged woman sitting in the front seat with a cheesy grin plastered on her face. "Gee, Curtis, that's nice of you, but I'd rather walk."

"It's Kevin."

I nodded, not really listening to him. "That's nice." I needed him to leave so I could use the zap home app my dad put on my phone. "I like walking in subzero temperatures, and it's still light enough to see a few feet in front of me."

"Are you sure? Because it's really no problem."

Judging by the determined look in his eye, he wasn't going to give up. At this rate, it would be faster to go with him, and I wouldn't get frostbite waiting for him to leave. "Fine."

He opened the front door of the car for me and reached behind him to roll down the back window. "You can sit in the front. The back door doesn't work." Then he crawled in the backseat through the open window.

I sniffed. The car smelled like stale cheese fries and puppies. What if a puppy had been on that seat? Puppies aren't known for having bladders of steel. "I hate to put you out." I stepped back. There was an alley nearby. If I ran fast enough, I could duck in there and hit the app before Columbus could climb back out of the window. The taste of slug slime filled my mouth. I climbed in the front seat before the actual slug arrived and sat as far forward as humanly possible. "Which is why I'm so grateful you stopped for me." I gave them my best impression of my mom's smile.

Carmichael's mom must have been a cheerleader, back when she was young. She somehow oozed spirit and joy. Cheermom twisted her key and hot air blasted from the heater vents. I leaned back but not too far back. "It's pretty toasty in here."

Cheermom had to yell so I could hear her over the blasting vent. "We have to have the heater turned all the way up so the car doesn't overheat."

It was January, and I had a river of sweat flowing down my face. "Do you mind if I roll the window down?" I yelled over the howling wind.

She shook her head. "That window doesn't work."

I should have gone with the slime. Slugs don't leave anything that good toothpaste can't rinse out. Heatstroke, on the other hand, can lead to death, which doesn't wash away.

"Where do you live, dear?" Cheermom's smile never wavered.

"Perilous Manor."

Now her smile wavered. I love my home and the look of horror it puts on other people's faces.

"Perilous Manor? I didn't know people actually *lived* there." She said it like she expected people to do something else.

"It's not perfect, but it's home." I ignored the urge to tell her where Amy lived.

"I thought it was condemned."

"Mom!" Charles buried his face in his hands. "Please stop talking about Raven's home."

Cheermom did her best to resurrect her smile. "So you're a Perilous."

I matched her insincere smile. "Yes, I am." She pulled up next to my house. I got out of the car and waved. "Thanks for the ride, Capulet."

Cheermom was probably forbidding him through gritted teeth to ever see me again as she waved good-bye.

# Five

My feet left small indents in the frozen snow that buried our driveway. Dad's favorite method of transportation didn't involve cars, so he didn't see the point in shoveling. I noticed Cheermom didn't wait to see if I got inside safely. That should be the last time Camden offers me a ride.

The front door creaked open on its own. Sunlight penetrated a few feet into the darkened hallway. I couldn't see anything in the gloom.

"Anyone home?" I stuck my head through the doorway and squinted in the dark. Where did the windows go? Maybe I should have apologized to the house for knocking the mace over. I stepped over the threshold, and the door swung at me. I jumped out of the way as it slammed shut. It was pitch black. The scent of burnt toast still hung in the air.

"Sorry about the floor." I ran my hand along the wall, searching for a light switch and finding cold stones instead of tapestries. The floor sloped down. "Good idea, house. I bet there's a nice rug in the basement that can cover that little hole." I usually refer to the basement as the dungeon, but I didn't want to give the house any ideas.

I kept my hand on the wall until I ran into a cold metal door. "Mom!" I yelled. The door opened, and I fell head-first into the dungeon. Fortunately, Mom's fluffy towel collection was next to the door, so I had a soft landing.

"I said I was sorry," I yelled to the house. The dungeon door slammed behind me. "Some light would make it easier to find that rug." At this point, I doubted the house was interested in a rug, but it didn't hurt to hold out hope.

A dim light appeared ahead of me. I stumbled through stacks of fire pokers and crashed into another door. The light was coming from a keyhole in the doorknob. I hesitated before opening the door. It was the kind of door that would hide a spinning wheel with a glowing spindle. I was too young to sleep away the next hundred years. The door opened, and I breathed a sigh of relief. It was my bedroom.

"Not funny," I yelled to the house. A rolled-up rug leaning against the wall fell over and shoved me into my room. The door slammed shut behind me. I pounded my fist on it. "It was a tiny hole! You're self-repairing." I grabbed the doorknob, and it opened, but not to the basement. An icy wind blew in and ruffled some loose pages on my desk. The Forbidden Woods spread out far below me. My bedroom had become a tower. Great.

I couldn't rappel down the side since I didn't keep rope in my bedroom, which was really stupid on my part. I slammed the door and sat on my bed to pout. "My dad won't let you get away with this."

A small tray appeared on my bedside table. It contained burnt toast and a glass of water. My house had the dumbest sense of humor. I grabbed my backpack and spent a fun-filled evening doing homework.

The house provided me with a cold bucket of water and a real flushing toilet. Then it made up for its generosity by cutting back on the heat. I put my fluffy pink kitten pajamas on. They looked dumb, but they were the warmest pajamas I had.

My stomach growled. I dialed Dad's number.

"How's my Raven?"

"The house turned my bedroom into a tower, Dad. My worst nightmare came true."

Dad laughed. "It was a pretty big gouge you left in the hallway. The house refinished the hardwood floors last week. You should have been more careful."

"Are you siding with the house?"

"You also hurt your mom's feelings."

"But I'm starving."

A plate of real food appeared on the bedside table. "I'll send up some climbing gear tomorrow morning so you can go to school." Then he hung up.

"Nice."

I ate quickly so the house couldn't mess with my food.

The lights dimmed.

"It's only eight thirty," I informed the house. "I don't go to bed this early."

The lights went out.

Moonlight filtered through my window and cast shadows from the Forbidden Woods on my wall. Something rustled by my bed. I swallowed. The house couldn't be *that* mad. I mean, I'd done worse than a little hole in the floor. I swallowed harder. Death by angry magic house was not how I wanted to go. Actually, I didn't want to go at all. I had plans to become an evil auditor for the IRS.

Two glowing red eyes appeared on my pillow, watching me. I backed away.

"Nice house monster," I whispered, tripping over my backpack. "Please don't eat me."

"I'd rather eat cheese," the monster squeaked.

"Cheese?"

The lights flickered back on. There, on my bed, sat Charming in small rat form.

I put my hand over my pounding heart. "When Amy said her spell was temporary, she really meant it."

"I'm slightly relieved. Her magic is rather uncontrolled." His voice sounded strange, coming from a rat.

"I didn't know you could talk in rat form."

"We're locked in a magical tower. Rats can always talk in magical towers. Just don't expect me to make you a dress or anything."

Ew. I couldn't think of anything more revolting. "I'm not into dresses. Do you have to sit on my pillow?" I couldn't sleep on a rat-infested pillow.

"I didn't come here on my own. I was exploring your strange village, looking for a way back into the Enchanted Forest, when I suddenly turned back into a rat and appeared on your pillow."

"But I never agreed to let you come home with me." I grabbed my trusty book of fairy tales and opened to the princess and the frog story. "Look. It's a frog, not a rat."

"And you are more evil witch than princess." He twitched his whiskers.

"The princess has to agree to let the frog," I paused, "or rat, sleep in her room in exchange for him getting her golden ball from the well. I don't even own a golden ball." Mom's fairy godmother gave one to me once, but I promptly threw it away.

He shrugged. "I'm not the one in control." He turned around in a little circle. "Nice pillow. Very soft."

I opened my door. Frigid air blew my hair in every direction. I shut the door. The screen on my phone read: *Communication privileges revoked*. We were stuck in here for the night. I moved my pillow, with the rat, to the window seat. We could get out in the morning. The house wouldn't keep me away from school, especially when there were more butterfly poems to hear.

"You can sleep here tonight. I'll ask my dad for help tomorrow," I said. I wasn't excited about helping Charming, but I would do anything to get rid of him. He couldn't stay in my room forever. He was a boy. Ew.

He sat up on his hind legs and glared at me with his beady red eyes. "You will do no such thing. I will not ask your father for help. You got me into this mess. You can get me out."

"I did not get you into any mess. I'm not a witch. I can't control magic, and you've seen the kind of magic Amy does. There is no way she could have pulled this off."

"Then who could be responsible?"

"That's why I wanted to ask my dad for help." I didn't know anyone else who knew about magic, other than my mom's fairy godmother, and she was kind of flighty.

"No." He turned his furry white back to me and snuggled into my pillow. I was never going to use that pillow again. "Do you have a box?"

"Why?"

"I don't like being out in the open like this."

I plopped an old shoe box on the pillow. He scurried under the box, leaving his naked little tail sticking out. It looked like a worm. Ew. "Anything else?"

"You could remove your evil spell."

"I would if it was my spell to remove." I sighed and buried my face in a decorative pillow. Mom would freak, but she seriously couldn't expect me to use a pillow that had been touched by a rat. Could my life possibly get any worse?

Charming cleared his throat. "Oh, and by the way, nice kitty jammies."

I hate my life.

# Six

The house didn't forgive me during the night. I awoke to a breakfast tray filled with burnt toast, runny eggs, and a climbing carabiner. My bedroom door opened to a frigid blue sky. Mist hovered over the ground, turning the trees into spikes rising from a vapid sea. Wind blew through the woods, knocking icicles into the mist and blowing hair in my face.

Charming's pink tail stuck out from under the shoebox and curled around the edge of my pillow. I let him sleep while I went to take care of some necessary business. My bathroom had returned, much to my relief.

The house wasn't the only thing that had changed during the night. My hair was about six inches longer. Sudden hair growth and a tower prison in one night. *If Charming ever tells me to let down my hair, I will strangle him with it.*

"Rise and shine, Charming." I put my books in my backpack and made sure I had enough money for lunch. As soon as I touched the carabiner, a rope shot out of it, and the eggs and toast blurred. When they came back into focus, the eggs were properly cooked, and the toast was smothered in butter and jam. I scraped the jam back. The toast wasn't burned. A big mug with steaming hot chocolate appeared next to the plate. My dad is the best sorcerer ever. He can even fix Mom's cooking.

I stuffed my mouth with scrambled eggs, followed by a swig of hot chocolate and a big bite of toast. "Charming? Wake up. It's almost time for school," I said through a mouthful of toast. "Want some breakfast?" Jam dripped down my fingers as I ripped a chunk of toast off for the rat. I hurried back to the bathroom and washed my hands and face. His tail was still in the same position when I returned. "Charming?"

Nothing.

I tiptoed over to the window. A small layer of frost covered his tail. "Charming!" I yelled. I yanked the box off the pillow. Charming didn't move. It was cold next to my window, but I didn't think it was *that* cold. I grabbed the rat and ran back into the bathroom.

"Don't be dead, don't be dead, don't be dead." I turned the water on warm and stuck Charming under it.

His snout opened, and his chest expanded. "H-h-h-h!"

"You aren't dead!" I switched the water temperature to tepid so he could thaw in comfort while I lectured him. "Why didn't you tell me it was too cold by the window? You have to tuck your tail inside the box to avoid freezer burn. Do you have any idea how disgusting dead rats can be?"

"I've never slept with a tail before." His teeth chattered as he talked.

A snowball hit my window. I opened it and looked out. "Time to go!" Edgar yelled from below.

I checked my phone. "We're going to be late for school."

I tucked Charming inside my backpack. "Don't worry. I won't leave you in the biology lab." I grabbed the rope, hooked the carabiner around my bed post, and tossed the other end out the window.

"Hurry, Raven! The bus is going to be here soon," Edgar said.

I climbed out the window, and the rope grew until I reached the ground. Then it recoiled like a tape measure, leaving only the carabiner in my hand. I hooked it to my pants, and the window slammed shut.

There was something spicy in the air. I sniffed. It was Edgar. "What is that smell?"

"The house turned my room into a grand palace last night. My bath water was scented this morning. How was the tower?"

"I slept in my own bed." He looked a little disappointed, so I added, "And it smelled a lot better than whatever the house did to you."

We skidded through the snow and got to the bus stop as the bus rolled up. I grabbed Edgar's arm before he could sit in his regular seat. "Sit with me today."

He raised a black eyebrow and moved to the back with me. "What's up?"

I unzipped my backpack. Charming must have had a hard time staying upright because he was on his back, his chubby white tummy sticking out.

"What is that?" Edgar poked Charming's furry middle. "Why are you carrying a rat?"

Charming rolled around in my backpack and bared his teeth at Edgar.

Edgar pulled his hand away from Charming. "You're getting to be more and more like Mom every day."

"I am not." I elbowed him since my hands were full. "The rat is not my friend. This is Prince Charming."

Edgar's jaw dropped. "No way. But I couldn't have done that. I was never in the same room with you two, except for during lunch, and I left before he got close. It isn't possible. Are you sure it's Charming?"

Charming glared at Edgar with his beady little eyes and squeaked.

"I'm sure." I zipped my backpack, muffling his squeaks. The bus pulled over to the side. I dropped my voice as other kids filled the aisles. "And why does it matter that you weren't with us?"

"Dad told me there could be a magical reaction if a prince charming ever showed up." He must have seen the blank look on my face because he continued. "It's all very scientific. You were the gunpowder. Charming was the fuse. All you needed was a spark." He pointed to himself. "Boom. Fairy-tale madness."

"How am I the gunpowder?" I asked.

"You probably said something stupid."

"It wasn't stupid. I said I'd rather kiss a rat. It was accurate, until he became a rat. Then it was even more repulsive. Besides, you weren't even with us."

"You must have had someone magical with you."

Amy climbed on the bus and made her way toward us.

Edgar scratched his chin. "Someone really bad at magic."

"Why would their ability to do magic make any difference?" I asked.

Edgar shrugged. "Because if they were any good at magic, they would have immediately done an undo spell."

Amy must have heard our conversation because she suddenly stopped walking toward us. Someone shoved her from behind so she slunk into the seat across the aisle from us.

"What's an undo spell?" I asked.

"Any idiot with magical abilities can do an undo spell," Edgar said. "It's an immediate reversal of a spell, like control-Z when you do something dumb on the computer." He noticed Amy sitting next to us, her whole body sparkling. "Wait a minute . . ." He didn't bother to hold back the laughter. "Amy?"

She pretended she didn't hear him.

"Hey, Miss Sparklepants?" he sang.

"Gosh darn it, Edgar. Do you think you could say it any louder? There might be some kids at the front of the bus who didn't hear you."

"Come on out, Charming." Edgar unzipped my backpack.

Charming glared at me from atop my math book.

Amy scooted over to our seat and peeked in my backpack. "Oh dear. It's not my fault. I haven't been trained." She took her wand from her backpack. "I can't undo the spell, but I can temporarily undo it again." Charming dove under my math book.

"Again? You've already tried?" Edgar grabbed Charming by the tail. "This I've got to see."

Amy repeated her crappy poem, and a furry Charming appeared out of nowhere onto our laps. His ears were high on his head and his nose was still rat-like. He'd left so quickly the night before that I didn't get a good look at him. Amy and I scooted out from under him and went across the aisle.

Edgar scratched his chin. "Your poem could use some work."

"No!" Charming said. Kids around the bus turned to look at us. He lowered his voice. "I don't want to see what else she can come up with."

"Maybe I shouldn't have done that on the bus," Amy whispered.

"I don't think anyone noticed," I whispered back.

"Most people suffer from IRO," Edgar said. "Of course they didn't notice anything."

Charming's nose twitched.

"What's IRO?" I asked.

"The inability to recognize the obvious," Edgar said.

"Oh please." I rolled my eyes. "How could anyone be that oblivious? He's a giant rat."

"What about Little Red Riding Hood?" Edgar asked. "She didn't notice that her grandmother was a wolf."

"The wolf was wearing a hat," I said.

Edgar pointed to my head. "I bet you didn't notice your hair is pulling a Rapunzel."

Charming squinted at my hair. "Edgar's right. Your hair is getting longer. Although it isn't golden."

I ran my fingers through my hair. "I noticed."

"Sure you did." Edgar smiled and nodded at me.

"Getting locked in a tower stimulates hair growth," I said. Edgar continued to smile and nod at me like an idiot. "Should you be sitting with us, Edgar? Maybe you boys should move to the front of the bus, since you're such good friends now."

"The fuse has already blown." Edgar leaned back into the seat. "Now I get to sit back and enjoy the show."

"Or Raven could just kiss him and get it over with." Amy waved her hand with the wand in the air.

I ducked. "Watch where you're aiming that thing."

"Sorry." Amy tucked the wand into her backpack. "Maybe I should give up the wand."

I'd never seen her wand before the climbing gym. She used to carry an old nubby stick with her. "Where did you get it anyway?"

"Ummm." She pointed out the window. "Look! We're at school already. Can you believe how gosh darn fast we got here?" The brakes squealed as the driver turned into the drop-off zone. Amy grabbed her backpack and disappeared into the crowd of students headed for another joyful day at middle school.

# Seven

Amy was out of sight by the time I got off the bus and collected my shoe from the third step. I grabbed Charming's arm for balance and slipped my shoe back on. "You aren't planning to go to school like that, are you?" I asked, looking around.

His nose twitched. "I like school. Back home I only got to study sword fighting and gallantry. Yesterday I learned about proper nutrition and solved for X."

"Yes, but . . ." I looked around to make sure no one was listening to us. "You're furry."

"No one will care."

"You can't seriously think this IRO thing will keep people from noticing you're an overgrown rat." I'm not sure why I cared. I mean, he was the enemy, but I couldn't help feeling bad for him. It wasn't his fault he was destined to be a prince charming, just unfortunate DNA. I knew all about unfortunate DNA.

He grinned. His front teeth were longer than the others and just a tad yellow. "Watch this." He scurried over to a girl from another bus. "Hey."

The girl's smile grew until it covered half her face. She could have benefited from a well-trained orthodontist. "Oh, hi . . . Eric." She let out this high-pitched squeal that was probably supposed to be a giggle.

"Raven here thinks I look unwell today," he said, pointing at me. "How do you think I look?"

The girl's jaw dropped open, and she let out something that sounded like a stuck pig. "I think you look stunning." Then she tripped over the curb. Charming caught her before she landed in the slush—which would have made my morning. Curse his gallantry.

"Careful. There's a nasty step there." He grabbed her backpack and helped her up the icy curb. I may have thrown up a little in my mouth.

Edgar joined me on the freshly shoveled ramp.

"Maybe she'll kiss him so I won't have to," I said.

"Not a chance, sis," Edgar said, opening the school door. "Even if she does kiss him, it won't break the spell. He needs a genuine princess or true love."

I braced myself for the stench that was middle school and followed Edgar inside. "Are you sure? Whatever is going on here isn't following any fairy tale I've heard of. It's the princess and the frog, not the princess and the rat."

"True love's kiss, the kiss of a princess or prince. That stuff is timeless."

Timeless and disgusting. "Fairy tales could use some updating. What's wrong with the commoner and the rat?"

Edgar and I maneuvered through the crowded halls to our lockers. "Why don't you just kiss him and get it over with?" Edgar asked. "The poor guy is suffering."

"Since when did you care about someone else's suffering?"

"Since he attached himself to our family. He won't be going away until you lay a juicy one on him."

I pretended to not hear that last line. "He didn't look like he was suffering when he was helping that girl over the icy curb."

"His eyes are permanently dilated."

"I'm not going to kiss him, Edgar." I opened my locker and tossed my backpack inside. I shuddered. The thought of kissing a boy was just . . . ew. I'd seen way too many boys eat dirt to even consider it.

Edgar snorted. "Then I guess you'll have to get used to having him on your pillow at night."

"This isn't fair. He's Mom's prince charming, not mine. How did he get to be my problem?"

Edgar tilted his head to the side. "Charming is Mom's Charming?"

The bell rang. "Dad cursed him and sent him into the future so he's stuck here." On my pillow. In my room.

"We'll have to tell Dad. He's been waiting for Charming to show up. He's why Dad never fenced in our backyard."

"We're going to be late." I hurried off to class. Amy wasn't there yet so I sat in the back under the Jabberwocky poster. The toothy beast above my head was soothing. Charming sat in the front. Amy still hadn't arrived when the second bell rang. I watched the door for a sparkly girl with a wand. Where was she?

The vice principal stormed into the classroom before Mrs. Anders could take roll.

"I need Raven Perilous and Amaryllis Featherfoot." She looked down at Charming and sighed. "You might as well come too."

"Amy—er, Amaryllis—isn't here yet," I said. I caught Charming's eye and raised my eyebrow. He shrugged.

Charming and I hung back from Ms. Darkwing as we followed her through the hall. Being forced to follow an authority figure had created an unspoken truce between the two of us.

"Were you expecting Ms. Darkwing to take us out of class?" I whispered.

"Ms. Darkwing?" Charming squeaked. "Her name is Ms. Darkwing?"

Ms. Darkwing turned. "Don't dawdle, children. Come along."

I hurried to catch up. Charming grabbed my arm and pulled me back. Even with furry skin and an elongated nose, Charming was still pretty cute—not that I noticed. "She has a villain name, Raven."

"I do too. It's just a coincidence."

"You can't tell me your name is a coincidence."

"Not my name. Ms. Darkwing's name."

"Ms. Darkwing can do magic."

He wasn't listening to me. "She's the vice principal, not an evil witch," I said.

"She's carrying a wand."

The stick in her hand could be mistaken for a wand, but it was too short and obviously broken. "Why would a vice principal carry a wand?" He wasn't seeing reason at all. "You didn't think she was an evil witch yesterday when she brought you to class."

"That's because I didn't know her name. She met me in the Forbidden Woods, gave me some clothes, and escorted me here. I never asked her name."

"I guess *you* were never warned against talking to

strangers in the woods," I said. My mom reminded me to never talk to strangers in the woods when she tucked me in at night. I used to have nightmares about talking to strangers.

Ms. Darkwing appeared behind us. She could move fast for an old lady. I didn't even see her go around us. "Come along, children." She grabbed our arms and dragged us into a nearby supply room. Tables lined the room, and chairs were stacked higher than my head. The far wall was obscured in darkness. Ms. Darkwing locked the door and glared down her beaky nose at us. "Where is Amaryllis?"

"I haven't seen her since she got off the bus," I said.

"Hmm." She eyed me for a moment. Then she aimed her broken stick at me. "Princesses should never wear ripped jeans," Ms. Darkwing said. White sparks flew out of the stick and surrounded me. When they cleared, my jeans and T-shirt had turned into a fluffy blue dress with an attached white apron. To make matters worse, it sparkled. I looked like a walking rhinestone.

I screamed, "Get this off of me!" I yanked at the frilly apron, but it wouldn't come off. Charming snorted in a very ungallant manner.

Ms. Darkwing shook her wand. "That wasn't what it was supposed to do. I was trying to fix your rip."

"Charming was right. You are a witch." I wasn't sure if I should be more horrified about Charming being right or about my vice principal being an evil witch. I looked down and realized that I was wearing white tights. It was too much for me, and not just because white tights looked terrible with my sneakers. I stomped my foot. "I want my normal clothes back. Although, I wouldn't mind different shoes. Have you seen the ones Amy wears? Those are cute."

Charming snorted again. His ears turned bright pink as he laughed at my expense.

Ms. Darkwing shook her broken wand again. "I need some help here." She closed her eyes and scrunched her eyebrows. "Where could Amaryllis have gone?"

Something in the back of the room thumped. Charming moved to protect me, but my massive skirt wouldn't let him near me. The entire room shook with the next thud. Chairs fell around us. I considered letting Charming hold me, but only for a second.

A huge figure smashed through a stack of chairs and lumbered toward us. It was the old lumberjack mascot, a fifteen-foot-tall wooden statue with an ax as big as me. The school board had retired it due to the zero tolerance policy. Its head was carved too large for the body, and its creepy smile took up half the face. The paint was faded and flaking off. Only one eye remained, giving it a perpetual wink.

The lumberjack creaked as it reached out for me. I ducked behind Charming, so it grabbed us both.

Ms. Darkwing's eyes were still closed. She shook her broken stick. "It's hard to concentrate when you two are making so much noise. This wand is hopeless. Surely you have some idea where Amaryllis went?"

"I don't know," I said, struggling to free myself. "You can't force information out of us that we don't have. Let us go!" My skirts were so big, I couldn't see anything but fluffy blue.

Charming struggled next to me. "Death by skirts! What a way to go."

I would have slugged him if I had known where my arms were. The lumberjack turned and thundered back into the dark end of the room. Ms. Darkwing shouted something, but I couldn't hear over the thundering steps of the lumberjack.

A motor whirred, and it suddenly grew brighter. Colder too.

"Where is it taking us?" Charming yelled. "It just opened some kind of door."

I opened my mouth and got a mouthful of skirt. I spit it back out. "How should I know? I can't read its mind."

"It's a statue. It doesn't have a mind."

"Exactly." I squirmed away from the skirt in my face. There was nothing on this side of the school but the gate to the Forbidden Woods.

The lumberjack crunched through the snow. A crooked *No Trespassing* sign hung over the gate. The lumberjack kicked the gate open, but it was too big to fit between the posts. It stood there for a moment and then tossed us in. We landed in a big pile of snow and skirts in the Forbidden Woods.

# Eight

I scrambled to my feet. A warm red cloak appeared out of nowhere and settled on my shoulders. It wouldn't come off either, which was just as well since I was freezing. Charming pulled the hood over my head. I pushed it off.

"We have to get out of here," I said. The lumberjack planted itself in front of the broken gate, blocking our exit. "Out of my way, you overgrown toothpick."

Charming brushed snow off his pants. "I don't think it's going to move. Why would it bring us here?"

"It's being controlled by a witch, Charming. Witches have an obsession with putting damsels in distress." I swallowed to keep control of my voice. "Do you have any idea what happens to girls who go into the Forbidden Woods?"

He shrugged.

"Little Red Riding Hood?" I tugged on my hood to illustrate.

"The wolf ate her grandmother, not her. You don't even have a grandmother."

"I do too." My mom lost track of her parents after she was kidnapped, but Grandma Perilous sends Edgar and me a birthday present every year. Last time it was a cockroach. Even Edgar was disgusted, and he's a boy. I hid in my room until my dad disposed of it. "She's not exactly the type of grandmother one visits, though."

Charming took a deep breath, which was a little freaky because he did it exactly the same way Mom does when she's frustrated with me. "You aren't going to visit your grandmother," he said slowly. I wondered if he'd hit his head or something.

"Snow White was taken captive by seven little men and turned into a slave." I spoke slowly too, but not because I thought he might be having cognitive trouble. I did it just to annoy him. His furry ears turned pink. Mission accomplished.

"The dwarves were her friends. Besides, those girls didn't have Prince Charming with them in the woods." He turned on his charmer smile, which isn't as effective with oversized yellow teeth.

"Lucky girls." I half expected my high level of sarcasm to generate a slug, but Amy must have cancelled the spell on the bus. She wasn't completely hopeless with magic.

His smile never wavered. "And Gretel did have Hansel."

"They were brother and sister." A howl echoed from somewhere deep in the woods. Mist crept over the path, covering our prints in the snow. "There is a deadly beast in the woods."

Charming's smile vanished. "Now that is something to worry about." He broke a branch off a nearby tree. "I really miss my sword."

"What happened to it?"

"Your dad took it," he said, scowling. "He said I could hurt someone with it."

"Oh yeah." I kept forgetting that he was part of my parents' past and that my dad was the bad guy, although Dad did have a point. Swords are dangerous. I wasn't allowed to play with them either.

Branches snapped. Something big was moving through the forest. We had to get out of there. I tiptoed to the gate, but the moment I touched it, the lumberjack reached for me.

"Where does this path go?" Charming asked.

"It leads to my house."

"Isn't that on the other side of the woods?"

I nodded. "There are only two ways in or out of the woods, unless . . ."

"Unless what?"

"I think there's an entrance to the Enchanted Forest in here somewhere."

"I can't go back there until I find my true love."

The Enchanted Forest was definitely out. I searched for pockets, hoping to find my phone tucked in among all my skirts. No luck. The beast howled again. It was getting closer. "We'll have to go to my house."

"The house that turned your bedroom into a tower?"

"I only have one house. Besides, it was kind of mad at me."

"I'd hate to visit when it's *really* mad at you."

We left the lumberjack guarding the gate as we followed the path to my house. The thick snow crunched under our feet as we ducked under icy branches and stepped over protruding roots. The howling got closer. I found myself inching nearer to Charming, despite my massive skirt.

My braid caught on a branch just as my backyard came into view. I yanked, but it didn't come free.

"Come on, Raven," Charming grabbed my arm. "I can see your house."

"My hair is stuck."

Yellow eyes appeared in the mist. I yanked harder. The braid looped around the branch and snaked off into the trees. "Where is my hair going?" I screamed.

"I think you mean, where is it growing?"

"Not funny, Charming." I held my breath so I wouldn't cry.

I could hear the beast *breathing*.

Charming stood between me and the beast, bravely (or should I say foolishly?) waving his stick. I screamed at the top of my lungs.

The back door opened, and my dad stepped out onto the back porch. "Raven!" He ran toward us but did a double take when he saw Charming and the beast. He turned and vanished inside the house.

"Daddy!"

A toothy snout appeared from behind a tree. Its breath came out in white puffs.

"Your dad abandoned you?" Charming looked as shocked as I felt.

"No. He wouldn't."

The back door opened again, and Dad ran out with a sword in one hand and a flame in the other. I knew he would never abandon me. "Catch!" He tossed the sword. It flashed in the sun before landing in Charming's hand.

"My sword!" He held the sword up to the sunlight and grinned like an idiot. Then he lowered the sword and scurried back to my side. For a moment there I thought he was going to kiss the thing and leave me to the beast.

"Cut her hair!" Dad yelled as he ran toward us.

Charming lifted his sword and brought it down on my braid. It bounced back like my hair was made of armor, which was wrong on so many levels. "It won't cut."

Dad reached my side. Sparks flew between his fingers. "I can protect my daughter."

"I'm not leaving." Charming swung his sword as the beast lurched toward us.

"Why?" I tugged on my hair, even though I knew it wouldn't do any good. "You don't even like me."

"Because I'm Prince Charming." He sounded more scared than noble. "It's not in my blood to leave a helpless girl to a beast."

"Helpless?" I went to kick him but was blocked by Dad's foot.

"Not a good idea, Raven." He waved his hands over my hair. A blue aura appeared around us. My braid continued to crawl through the dirt as it grew longer. No amount of shampoo would ever remove all the filth. "Magic won't cut it either."

"The fairy tale is all wrong," Charming said. "She's supposed to still be in the tower so her knight in shining armor can climb her hair and rescue her. The whole story line has been broken since she rappelled down to go to school. How can anyone climb her hair when she's on the ground?"

"I don't need rescuing." I stretched my leg out as far as it would go. That beast was toast if it ever got close enough. If I couldn't kick it, I would smother it in my skirt.

Dad glanced down at Charming and did another double take. "I don't understand. Why are you still so young? And . . . why are you furry? That wasn't part of my spell."

Charming didn't answer because the dark beast lunged at him, teeth bared. It was as big as Charming, and just as hairy, but not as cute. Charming lashed at it with his sword, hitting the beast's nose. Blood oozed from the wound and the beast backed into the trees, leaving a red trail behind it.

"It won't stay back for long," Charming said.

I'd never seen a rat fight like that before. "Who knew vermin could be so heroic?" I said. If I had a sword, I would have been beating the beast too, except for the part where I was tied to a tree with my own hair. Have I mentioned how much I hate my life?

Dad got one of those looks on his face that couldn't be good, especially not when matched with the word vermin. "That's it!" He pointed at me. Once again—not good.

Burnt toast crumbs appeared in my hair. "Ew, Dad. What did you do that for?"

Dad didn't answer. He swept his hand in an arc, and a trail of burnt toast crumbs appeared, leading from my feet to the back porch.

Something scurried out from under the porch and stopped at the first crumb. "What is that?" It scuttled closer. "Dad?" Its antennae swiveled, and I swear it looked straight at me.

"I didn't have the heart to flush that cockroach my mother sent you kids for your last birthday. There was something about it . . ."

My mouth was open, but no scream came out. I snapped it shut when the cockroach launched into the air.

"He's a really well-behaved cockroach," Dad continued. "Look how shiny his shell is. A cockroach with a shiny shell is as close as we got to a knight in shining armor. It should be enough to break the spell that won't let us cut your hair before the beast returns."

The cockroach landed on my hair. I did what any girl in my situation would do. I frantically tried to rip my hair out, which hurt and didn't help at all. The cockroach scurried toward my head, munching on burnt crumbs as it went.

An angry howl filled the air. The beast had crept around us and lunged from behind. Charming slashed at the beast, cutting the tip of its ear off. It backed away from Charming's sword with a snarl and cut us off from my dad.

"Hold still." Charming slashed my hair with his sword as soon as the cockroach reached my shoulder. Thankfully, he severed my hair above the cockroach.

I stepped away from the tree, hoping there wasn't any beast blood in my hair. "Dad, zap it with magic."

A second beast appeared next to Dad.

"I'll hold this one back," Dad said. "Can you handle the first one, kid?"

Charming nodded.

Dad zapped the beast next to him with fire bolts. "Raven, you go inside. Charming and I will deal with the beasts."

"You're going to work together?" I asked. "Aren't we supposed to be enemies?"

The new beast turned toward me. Charming grabbed my arm and pulled me to him as it lunged for me. The first beast snarled. We backed away.

"Raven!" Dad yelled, his face full of panic. "Kids! Don't back up any more."

It was too late. We stepped back one more time. The beasts and the snowy woods vanished. Charming and I found ourselves in a green clearing dotted with daisies and sunflowers. Lofty trees surrounded the meadow, their strong branches held open like welcoming arms. It would have felt like paradise, had one of the paths not led to a cottage made of gingerbread.

We'd found the entrance to the Enchanted Forest.

# Nine

The gingerbread house smelled sweet, but stale. A big chunk of frosting was missing from the roof and some of the gumdrops were missing in the front, leaving colorful indentations where they once were. Charming took a few steps forward. I grabbed his arm and yanked him back. "Seriously?"

"I wasn't going to eat anything." Charming inspected my hair. "I cut that surprisingly straight."

"I'm a princess. Bad haircuts are impossible." I took a deep breath. The dirty hair and cockroach were gone. Everything was going to be okay.

He wasn't listening to me. He was eyeing the gingerbread house. "The windows are made out of hard candy. I wonder if it's cinnamon."

I'm pretty sure he drooled a little. What is it with boys and their stomachs? Although, I had to admit, the chocolate front porch looked delicious, at least from a distance. It was probably old and stale. "Knock it off. We have to find a way back to the real world."

Charming shook his head. "Not me. I'm home."

"But you were cursed. Don't you have to go back and find your true love?" Then I realized his curse was that he couldn't return until he found his true love—and I was the only girl with him. Charming looked at me. I think he realized it too. Suddenly, my red cloak was too warm.

"Maybe all the funky magic in the air cancelled the curse and sent me back." He stared at a spot next to my feet.

"My dad couldn't have been that great at magic when he was seventeen. That must have been it." I searched for something else to talk about and noticed a small rock on the ground. "Oh, look—a rock!" I picked it up and tossed it to him. "You never know when a rock will come in handy."

"Rocks are good." He put the rock in his pocket. "One can never have too many . . . rocks."

I stared at the gingerbread house, not really focusing on the silhouette in the sugar pane window. "So you have your sword back."

"True." He held his sword up in the sunlight. "It's too bad I don't have my scabbard too."

"I bet we could find something that would help you carry it."

Charming pointed to something behind me. "What's that?"

It was my magical dirty hair. The braid must have come through with us. Gross. I traced the path of the braid with my finger. "Look! The braid disappears. That must be the way back!" We hurried to the place where my hair vanished and ran into Edgar as he appeared. There was a hiss, and the braid rolled to the side like a severed head. The exit had closed behind Edgar.

"How did you get here?" Edgar and I asked at the same time. Synchronized talking. It's a twin thing.

"And what are you wearing?" I asked. Edgar was dressed in gym shorts and a T-shirt that had Perilous written in permanent marker on the front and back. "It's the middle of winter."

"Actually," Charming said. "We're in Summerland. It's never winter here."

"I was talking about home. It's winter where we came from." I glared at Charming, but he was too busy gazing at his stupid shiny sword to notice.

Edgar straightened his shirt, which did nothing for his pathetic fashion statement. If only those silly cheerleaders could see him now. "I was in gym, and a door to a storage closet opened all by itself."

"Please don't tell me you went to investigate," I said. (Our twin thing only went so far.)

"I didn't go to investigate. I went to shut the door."

I groaned.

"It was letting cold air into the gym. I was already cold enough wearing these stupid shorts. The old school mascot was waiting and dragged me to the Forbidden Woods. I got there in time to see you vanish and help Dad get rid of a beast. Then I tripped over a braid and ended up here. But why are you lecturing me about *my* clothes when you look like a stick of sparkling cotton candy?"

I'd forgotten about the dress of hideousness. "Ms. Darkwing is an evil witch. She magically turned me into a dork."

"Oh please," Charming said. "You can't blame that on Ms. Darkwing."

Edgar snorted. "Good one, Charming."

"That was rude." I put my hands on my hips and glared at him, which may have made me look even dorkier. "What kind of Prince Charming says stuff like that?"

Charming's nose twitched. "What do you expect?" His last word ended in a high-pitched squeal. "You turned me into a rat."

"I did not turn you into a rat!" I took a deep breath to let him have it but was cut short by a creaking door. The only door nearby was on the gingerbread house, and we all knew who lived there.

"Run!" I yelled. I took off for the trees, but no one followed me. The boys had apparently decided that they could handle the witch. I couldn't hide while they fought, so I went back and stood behind them. I should have spent less time learning how to climb walls and more time learning how to use a sword. I resolved then and there to get a sword at my earliest convenience.

A shadow appeared in the doorway. "I'll act as bait and talk to her," I whispered. "The witch is blind so she won't know how many of us there are. She's only expecting two. Charming, you come at her from the left. Edgar, hit her with a spell on the right."

"I am not using a girl as bait." Charming's nose twitched. "No matter how much she deserves it."

"You are infuriating." Heat rushed into my face, which meant it was probably bright red. It was time to let him have it.

"You know," a familiar voice said from the gingerbread house. "If I really was the witch, I could have captured, baked, and eaten you by now." Amy stepped out from the shadows.

"Amy?" I gasped. "You're the wicked witch that lives in the gingerbread house?"

"I'm not a wicked witch." For some reason, she sounded like she was trying to convince herself more than us.

Charming snorted and looked at me. "Where have I heard that before?"

"I'm not a witch, Charming," I said. I did my best to make my voice sound venomous, but I'm not sure how it came across with me dressed in sky-blue ruffles and a pretty red cape.

"Hansel and Gretel shoved the evil witch into the oven years ago. I've been staying here to be close to the school. It's a great place to practice magic." She opened the door and motioned for us to go inside. "Come on in. I have some freshly baked cookies."

"Wait," Charming said. "How do we know you're really Amy, and not an evil witch pretending to be Amy?"

"Gosh darn it, Eric. You know it's me." Red sparkles erupted from her ears.

Gosh darn, it was Amy. "I'm convinced," I said and went inside the house. Edgar and Charming followed.

"How do we know we're safe from Amy?" Edgar whispered to Charming.

"I heard that," Amy said.

My brain almost went into sugar overload from the smell alone. I sat on a pink sponge cake sofa and breathed in the strawberry scent. Amy set a plate of gingerbread men on the toffee table and sat next to me.

I eyed the cookies. "You, um, didn't bake them in your oven, did you?" A gingerbread wall painted with delicate pink frosting was all that separated us from the kitchen where Hansel and Gretel had baked the witch. Ew.

Amy nibbled the foot off a gingerbread man. "No. That oven is way too big for me to use. I bought these from the muffin man."

"Does he still live on Drury lane?" Charming grabbed a

cookie and sat on a giant muffin stool. The scent of blueberries filled the air.

"Yes, but it's not the same muffin man you knew. The old one retired last year and let his son take over."

Charming paused mid bite. "But his oldest son is close to my age. Ferran can barely cook a pancake."

"He's twenty-five. All the milkmaids are in love with him. He's cute, but I don't see what the fuss is. He's so old."

Charming dropped his cookie onto his lap, frosting side down. He didn't seem to notice. "We used to practice sword fighting together." His lip twitched.

Amy peeled the cookie off Charming's lap. "I'll get a rag for that."

That tiny spot in my chest ached again. Charming's life really was ruined. His friends were all grown up. Everyone he cared about probably thought he was dead. I poked at the couch to get my mind off Charming. One should not feel bad for the enemy.

Edgar wiped crumbs off his face. "So, Amy, I bet you have a real problem with ants." Trust Edgar to change a horrible subject to something equally horrible.

Amy grabbed a red-and-white striped washcloth from the kitchen and handed it to Charming. "The previous occupant put massive anti-ant spells on the house. I haven't seen one ant."

"So how do we get home?" Edgar asked.

"Amy goes back and forth all the time," I said. The sofa cushion crumbled under my fingers. I brushed the crumbs away, hoping that Amy wouldn't notice. "She can help us back."

Amy bit her lip and became very interested in her one-legged gingerbread man. "I can try, but I don't know if I can take you back."

"But we were going to do our nails here last night. Just send us back the way you would have sent me last night."

"Last night you were just my friend. I could have walked you home without any problems. This morning you're a princess in a strange land with a prince and an evil sorcerer."

"I feel so generic," Edgar whispered to Charming. Charming was apparently too shell-shocked to laugh.

"We may not have matching shoes, but I'm still your friend. Edgar's magic is only good for getting away with not brushing his teeth and Charming is . . . himself," I finished lamely.

A flame appeared in Edgar's hand. "My magic is good for fire too."

"I can try to take you home, but I don't think you'll be able to leave until you've completed a Quest."

"What Quest?" Edgar and I asked at the same time. (Twin thing.)

Amy broke the other leg off the gingerbread man. "Charming is still a rat."

I nodded in agreement until I realized she was talking literally. "Where are you going with this?"

Her eyes flickered to the front door before she leaned forward and whispered, "Kiss Charming and break the spell so you can go home."

That was all Charming needed to wake him from his stupor. He shook his head. "No kissing."

"Agreed." I glared at him. That was my line.

"Then maybe you need to find another princess to do the job," Amy suggested.

Charming scowled, but I thought it sounded like a great idea. "How convenient that we are suddenly in the land of fairy tales. We should be able to find someone to kiss him in no time. Then we leave him here with the lucky girl"—and by *lucky* I meant *super unfortunate*—"and I go home with Edgar."

"First, let's see if Amy can help you two get home," Charming said. "I can probably find someone to break the spell on my own."

Amy cleared her throat. "Uh, not a good idea." She took a deep breath. "In the Enchanted Forest, the strongest magic wins. My magic isn't even as strong as the rat spell. The good news is that you are kind of tied to Raven, magically speaking."

"How is that good news?" I asked.

Charming scratched his head. "What are you trying to say?"

"As long as Charming stays close to Raven, he won't turn all the way into a rat."

"How about you check on me now and then until I find a way to break the curse? If I'm a rat, then I'll let you do your spell."

Amy kicked a loose blueberry across the floor. It left a tiny blue trail in its wake. "The moment you leave Raven's side, you'll turn into a rat. And I kind of borrowed that wand from Ms. Darkwing. I'd get in a lot of trouble if she caught me with it, so I sent it back to her. I can't de-rat you without a wand."

# Ten

"Charming will turn into a rat if he doesn't stay by my side?" Panic squeezed up my gut and settled in my throat. How long was I going to be stuck with him? "But he'll be fine as soon as he finds a princess stupid enough to kiss him?" I blurted. Slime filled my mouth and something squirmed on top of my tongue. I gagged and spewed a frog. It jumped onto Charming's lap. Charming slumped on the couch and didn't seem to notice he had a slimy new friend.

I ran into the kitchen and rinsed my mouth out with soda water. Nothing in that house came without additional empty calories.

What I'd said was mean, even for me. No princess deserved to be stuck with Charming, no matter how stupid she was. Charming wasn't bad, as far as boys go, but he was still a boy. My stomach felt all twisted and strange. I filled my mouth with more soda water and swished it between my teeth before spitting it out in the sink.

Charming had looked so sad. I could have apologized to him, but that would have made me nice. I couldn't be nice in the Enchanted Forest, of all places. An empty tower was hidden somewhere in the forest, and I wasn't about to volunteer to fill it. It would be better for everyone if we found a way to break Charming's spell so I could go home to the real world.

I stumbled back and collapsed on the couch with the strawberry scent. The sweet smells that filled the house had lost their appeal.

Edgar had the frog on his lap. "Let's keep this one."

My tongue was too gross to use. I rested my head on my knees. Chances were good I would never speak again.

Amy cleared her throat. "Without the wand, I can't stop your frogs and slugs any more. You have to do good deeds or suffer the . . ." The frog expanded its throat and let out a *rrriiiibbit* ". . . consequences."

"You had Ms. Darkwing's wand all this time?" I asked, forgetting that my mouth was too disgusting to use. "How did she not notice her wand was missing all term?"

"I didn't have her wand all term. I found a way to misdirect the delivery of her new wand a little. I only had it a couple of days. My wand was old and broken. It let me cancel out your frogs and slugs, but it would never be strong enough to help Charming."

"You could try," Charming suggested.

Amy shook her head. "I sort of lost it."

"Ms. Darkwing had a broken old wand," Charming said. "I bet that's why she ordered a new one. She probably won't notice if it goes missing. It kind of worked."

"Excellent idea, Charming." I stood up and ran to the door. I could stand to be nice to him long enough to collect the broken wand, as soon as Amy could get us back to the real world.

We filed out of the gingerbread house with Amy in the lead. She stopped next to my severed braid and waved her hand in the air. Then she did some karate chop–type moves.

"What's wrong?" Charming asked.

"The entrance to the Forbidden Woods is right here." Amy pointed at nothing in front of her. "It won't open, and I can't force it without a wand. You're going to have to complete a Quest to get home."

"Step aside." Edgar cracked his knuckles and brought a flame up in his hands. "I don't need a wand to do magic." He reached forward. The air sizzled around his hands when he got to the end of my braid. He fell backward and landed on my severed hair. "Found the entrance. I think it's locked."

"You think?" A slug oozed out my mouth and dripped off my chin.

"That is disgusting, Raven," Charming said.

I couldn't even tell him off. It was so unfair. "I wish I had my own fairy godmother." I wilted onto the lawn, carefully avoiding the slug.

Blue sparkles appeared around us. The air filled with the scent of spicy citrus flowers.

"Gosh darn it," Amy whispered.

"What is it?" I asked.

My mother's fairy godmother appeared in front of us. "Hello, my dears."

"Lady Laurel!" Edgar said. "We're saved!"

"Finally," I said, never so happy to see an old pink-haired lady in my life, "someone who can save me from this fashion nightmare."

"Raven." Lady Laurel took one look at my dress and shook her head. "That dress will never do." She waved her wand and turned it pink.

"That's not really what I need." My mouth filled with slime. "I mean, it's lovely. The color is perfect." The slime vanished. So lying was allowed as long as it was nice lying. I resisted the temptation to roll my eyes. "But I would like my own clothes, please."

"Of course, dear." Lady Laurel waved her wand, and the fluffy dress of doom was replaced with my ripped jeans and black T-shirt.

I hugged my clothes. They felt wonderfully normal and not sparkly. "Thank you. Any chance you could do something with the frog and slug curse?"

Lady Laurel waved her wand over my head, and I felt instantly lighter.

"Charming is . . ." I paused, seized with the strange urge to not hurt his feelings again. "Charming is weird," I finished. No frogs. "Thank you, Lady Laurel."

"Hey!" Charming said. "That was rude."

"I know." But it wasn't as rude as it could have been. I hooked my thumbs in my belt loops and grinned. Normal clothes. No frogs or slugs. Fairy godmothers were the best. "Lady Laurel, could you please open the door so we can go home? We're missing school." I thought the school part was a nice touch.

Lady Laurel shook her head. "No, dear."

"What?" Edgar edged in closer. "What did you say? Because I thought you said no. Aren't you here to save us? I'm starving, and that house is not as edible as it looks."

"It's been there for a really long time," I said.

A light breeze wrapped us in the scent of stale gingerbread. Lady Laurel handed Edgar a dry biscuit, which looked as delicious as his naked toast. "I did say no, dear. You will have to find your own way out.

Fairy godmothers aren't supposed to meddle. Our job is to make sure you're properly dressed for the occasion and get you where you need to go." She shook her wand, and tiny blue sparks shot out of the end. "Now then, Amaryllis."

Amy popped out from behind me. "What?"

"Amaryllis, dear, I am disappointed in you."

Amy ran and threw her arms around Lady Laurel. "I know I didn't do what you asked. Things got complicated. Please forgive me."

Lady Laurel separated herself from Amy.

"She's been helping me," I said. "Frogs and slugs make terrible accessories. They're also hard to hide from the general populace." Mentioning good deeds should help her cause.

Amy smiled, but it wasn't her typical sparkly smile. I had a bad feeling that if I stomped on her toe, she'd just say ouch. "I borrowed Ms. Darkwing's new wand after you confiscated mine. I didn't think she'd notice."

Lady Laurel tapped her chin with her wand. Sparks swirled around them. "She noticed."

Charming cleared his throat. "Excuse me, but do you think you could help me?" His nose twitched. "My princess ran off with the witch's son, and he cursed me. Fourteen years went by while I was in limbo, and then their children turned me into a rat. My quest is over, and my life is ruined. I'm not even sure if my favorite moat monster is still alive." His left ear shuddered.

"You already have everything you need to help yourself," Lady Laurel told Charming. "You can all help Raven with the frogs and slugs by encouraging her to be good. Maybe you could pet some puppies." I groaned. It was like she didn't know me at all. "Once my blocking spell runs out, Raven will have to learn to be nice, or you will all be tripping over frogs and slugs."

"What?" I looked around the group in a panic. I could be nice to Amy, and maybe even Edgar, but Charming? "I was born to be evil. Nice isn't in my blood. And nice girls get locked in towers."

"Then you'll have to get used to the frogs and slugs, dear." She wasn't even trying to be sweet anymore.

"What about me?" Edgar asked. "I'm not really part of all this." He waved his hands in a circle to indicate the rest of us. (No brother-of-the-year award for him.)

Lady Laurel handed Edgar another biscuit. He got food. I got frogs and slugs. It's like everything was against me. "My dear Edgar. You could still be a great prince charming, with the proper training."

Edgar made a face that made him look like he'd swallowed a porcupine. Fortunately, my phone was still in my pocket, so I could take a picture. It was out of signal range, but that didn't affect the camera.

"Like Raven, I was born to be evil. Unlike Raven, I can back that up with magic." He sent an evil grin my way. "Don't you have some vague advice for me that I won't understand until it's too late?"

"Ah yes." Her eyes actually twinkled. "The tooth fairies are very impressed with your teeth cleaning spell." And then she was gone.

"You could have groveled a little more, Amy," Edgar said. "Maybe then she would have sent us home."

"She'll *never* send you home." She flicked her arm, and a short stick slid out of her sleeve. "I knew she was still carrying it."

"You pick-pocketed your own fairy godmother?" I asked, impressed.

"She isn't my fairy godmother," Amy said. She reached up and touched a sparkly flower jewel on her shirt. "Only princesses get a fairy godmother. The wand is broken, but I can use it for small spells." She didn't look at Charming.

We stared at each other for a while. We had an untrained fairy godmother who had nothing but a broken wand, an evil sorcerer who specialized in clean teeth and fireballs, a prince charming who looked like a rat, and me. I was the most normal of the bunch.

"So where do we go from here?" I asked. "Can you use the broken wand to get us home?"

Amy flicked her wand at the empty space where the door supposedly was, but nothing happened. "You can't go home until you fulfill the Quest."

Charming grabbed my severed braid and dragged it over to a tree stump. "I need a scabbard." He cut, snipped, and braided until he had a belt with a slot for his sword. It was weird, and not just because it was made out of my hair. It was also dirty.

"I think we need to find a princess for Charming," Edgar said. "Amy, you know the area. Where's the closest princess?"

Amy pointed at me.

I folded my arms. "Other than me."

"All paths lead to a village or a castle." She walked to a path that led into the woods. "This one leads to a small village. Beyond the village is a castle. There might be a princess there."

# Eleven

A small gray bunny hopped on the path in front
of us and paused, its fuzzy ears pointed in our direction. Chattering squirrels ran up and down the
trees all around us. The flowers looked like they were getting ready to burst into song. I wanted to go home to my
grumpy house.

"Hello, cute bunny," Amy said.

The bunny wiggled its nose, just like Charming. Then
it sniffed my leg. As tempted as I was, I didn't kick it. "Are
all wild animals so friendly here?"

"Only if they're cute." Amy patted the bunny's head.
"Wolves are beautiful in the regular world. Here, they're
ugly, vicious monsters."

A ball of flame appeared in Edgar's hand.

"Don't you dare torch the bunny, Edgar," Amy said.

The flame disappeared. Edgar ducked his head to hide
a grin. "I wasn't going to."

Amy turned her back to him and marched down the path.

My stomach growled. "Edgar, do you have any biscuits
left?"

Edgar shook his head and rubbed his belly. "Mmmm."

A bush rustled, and a small white kitten burst out of the foliage. It ran to Charming and hissed, swatting him with its tiny paw.

"It thinks you're really a rat," Amy said with a giggle.

"Smart kitten," I said. Puppies will never be fun for me, but I could come to like kittens.

Charming picked up the kitten. "It has a collar."

A little girl in a yellow dress ran down the path toward us, her golden curls bouncing with every step. "Angel! Oh, you found Angel." The girl grabbed the kitten and gave it a fierce hug. "You naughty kitten. You almost missed the wedding." She gave Charming a shy smile. "Thank you, kind rat-boy." She stood on her bare tippy toes and kissed his cheek. We all held our breath for a second, but the kiss didn't undo the spell.

"Rats," I mumbled. "I guess you aren't a princess." Of course she wasn't a princess. A princess wouldn't be out in public without shoes.

She shook her head. "No. I'm just Ella. Where are you going?"

"We're going to the castle," Amy said. "Who's getting married?"

"My father."

Something in my head clicked. A girl named Ella who couldn't keep shoes on her feet . . . "Your future step-mother doesn't happen to have two daughters about your age, does she?"

Ella nodded. "Yes. They don't talk a lot. I think they're shy. They're always whispering to each other. How did you know?"

"They're evil," I said. "I don't think they have your best

interest at heart, especially your future stepmother. You should tell your father you don't want him to die—er, I mean marry her."

Ella's eyes widened. "Die? My mother died when I was very little. I don't remember her." She turned and ran away with the kitten in her arms.

"Or at least have a lawyer make sure his will specifies you are the sole heir, and she's not your guardian," Edgar yelled. "Do you think she heard me?"

"I wonder if there's anyone who didn't hear." I rubbed my ear. Edgar had some powerful lungs. He would make a great lawyer one day.

"You two are pretty nice for a set of evil twins," Charming said.

"My motives are purely selfish," I explained. "Weren't you listening to Lady Laurel? I have to be nice to avoid the frogs and slugs."

Edgar shrugged. "I like messing with people's heads."

We walked for a few minutes before Lady Laurel appeared. Sparkles did not appear before her this time and her hair was slightly askew. "What are you doing here?" She shot an irritated look at Amy.

"Walking through the forest," Charming said.

"Of all the paths you could have taken, you chose the only one that doesn't lead to a princess. Ella's father just cancelled the wedding and is sending his formerly betrothed away with her two daughters."

"What's wrong with that?" I asked. "We just saved her from a super miserable childhood."

Lady Laurel shook her head. "Now Ella will never become Cinderella."

"Maybe Ella doesn't want to become Cinderella." I

know I wouldn't want to clean cinders from the fireplace. Ew.

Lady Laurel closed her eyes for a moment before speaking. "How about I help you out? There's a princess being held captive by a dragon in another part of the forest. Charming can rescue her, get his kiss, turn back into a prince, and you can all go home." She smiled brightly. "Sound good?" She waved her arm before we could answer, and the path vanished.

No one was surprised to appear on another path in what may or may not have been the same forest. The trees looked the same, but hey, they're trees. The flowers didn't look as cheerful, but again, flowers.

"So did Lady Laurel help us in our quest or just move us farther from the exit?" I asked. Her reaction to the whole Cinderella thing baffled me. It was like she wanted Ella to be miserable.

"Who cares?" Charming pulled his sword from his homemade hair scabbard (still weird). "There's a dragon to fight!" He grinned at his ratty reflection in the sword and ran up the path.

"You shouldn't run with pointy things!" I yelled after him. For those keeping score, that was my second helpful comment of the day. Mom would be choking out jewels if she'd been half so helpful.

Something roared down the path—from the opposite direction Charming ran. Edgar yanked Amy and me backward in time for Charming to come charging back down the path toward us, sword extended. He disappeared into the trees. Something roared again. We stared at the trees for a moment.

"I guess we could go help him," Edgar said with a sigh.

"Good idea," Amy said. "My wand can still manage clothes. I have the perfect dragon fighting outfit for you." Edgar's eyes widened. Somewhere in the distance, Charming screamed. Amy dug the broken wand out of her pocket, but Edgar had already vanished into the trees.

Black smoke rushed down the path toward us. We covered our mouths and stepped off the path. Charming seemed to know what he was doing with the sword, and Edgar was fireproof, but I still had a tiny knot in my stomach.

"Do you think the boys might need some help?" I peered around a tree but couldn't see anything through the thick smoke.

"You probably noticed how my other spells were less than perfect. I'm only good for accessorizing." A high-pitched scream joined the fray. "Guess they found the princess."

"And princesses are only good for screaming." I tapped my jeans with my open palms. There wasn't a sword for me, but I was more than a high-pitched squeal. I'd skipped an entire year of math. I had to be able to help somehow. Then I got a wicked idea. "What if you accessorized the dragon?"

Amy grinned, and we plunged into the thick smoke armed only with a broken wand and a couple of great minds that probably should have thought the situation through more thoroughly.

# Twelve

Amy and I hid behind a thick tree and surveyed
the scene. Bones were scattered everywhere, and
the stench of death was heavy in the air. Despite
the smell and general disgustingness of the area, both boys
were smiling.

Edgar formed a fireball in his hand and launched it
at the dragon. "Your mother was a gecko!" he yelled. The
flame went up the dragon's nose and fizzled out. The dragon's eyes watered, and it let out an explosive sneeze. Edgar
laughed as the flames curled around him. "You were right,
Charming. Fighting dragons is fun."

Charming dove at the dragon, deflecting his sword at
the last minute.

"You're supposed to stab it," Edgar said. He demon-
strated with a fiery hand. "It's why your sword is pointy."

"Dragon blood is corrosive," Charming said. "I don't
want to damage my sword."

"Stop chatting and insulting my mother!" the dragon
roared. "This is not a tea break!" It took a deep breath and
belched flames at them. Smoke rose from Charming's fur,

but he didn't burn. Edgar caught a few flames and juggled them. "Why won't you two die?" The dragon seemed to only have one volume—super loud.

"I'm a cursed prince." Charming rolled away from the dragon's sharp talons, jumped up, and stomped on its foot. "Princes only die tragically. Death is never tragic enough before a curse is broken. I can't get hurt as long as I'm a rat."

The dragon slapped Edgar's hand with his tail, forcing him to drop the flames. "And you?"

Edgar shrugged. "I'm a bad guy. We only die at the end. You should know that."

The dragon's tail snaked around the tree and wrapped around Amy and me. We never even saw it coming. I kicked but couldn't get free as the dark green coils squeezed. Screaming wasn't an option because I was not that kind of princess and also because breathing was difficult.

The dragon's laughter made his tail vibrate. "Why is a bad guy helping a good guy?"

Edgar launched a fireball at the dragon's face, narrowly missing a scaly green eye. "It's better than running laps in gym."

The dragon lifted Amy and me off the ground and held us up in the air. "I think I've found your weakness."

Edgar and Charming laughed. It was the most cheerful battle I'd ever witnessed. I, of course, was not laughing. That dragon smelled like death warmed over. The amount of germs I was getting exposed to made me shudder.

"Why are you laughing?" the dragon asked. "I'm going to eat them. Don't think I won't." He lifted us over his toothy maw. He had a shoe stuck between his teeth. Gross.

"They aren't as helpless as they appear," Charming said.

"And Sparklepants has a wand," Edgar added. "She's much scarier than you."

"Stop calling me that!" Amy yelled. She jabbed the dragon's tail with her wand. "Sunshine and daisies." Flaming red sparks erupted from the broken wand and surrounded us. The sparks circled the dragon and turned into an orange tutu. It looked especially lovely next to his green scales.

The dragon dropped us next to the boys. "Ack! What is this? Get it off me." He scratched at the tutu, but it didn't rip.

No one responded. We were all too busy laughing.

The dragon pumped his massive wings. Wind whipped hair around our faces as he lifted off. The bright orange tutu was visible until he vanished in the clouds.

"Oh, thank you," a shrill voice said from the dark cave. A girl stepped out. Her dress was torn and her cheeks were smudged black, but her hair was perfect. Typical princess. "You saved my . . ."—she paused when she saw our group— ". . . life?"

"No problem," Edgar said. "Do you know where the closest exit to the real world is? We're late for class."

"No." She knotted her eyebrows for a moment and then took hold of Charming's hand. "Thank you, noble prince, for saving me. Um, why are you a rat?"

Charming freed his hand from her grip. "The rat thing is complicated. What were you doing in the cave all that time? We had the dragon distracted. You could have run away."

"I was waiting for someone to rescue me." She fluttered her extremely long eyelashes. "You look pretty young." She puckered her lips and leaned toward Charming. He stepped backward before she could kiss him.

"I am young, and I didn't rescue you."

I elbowed him and whispered, "What are you doing? It's your chance to break the spell."

"It doesn't feel right," he whispered back. I blinked. Isn't kissing the damsel in distress his job? Wasn't that what he was trained for?

She turned to Edgar. "You don't look like a prince."

"Actually," I told her, "my brother *is* a prince, except our parents were banished."

"Brother?" The princess looked back and forth between us. I nodded. "You could kiss him."

"I'm really young too," Edgar said quickly. "In fact, I'm the same age as little Raven. We're twins. And I didn't really rescue you either. Amy did it." He pointed at Amy and hid behind Charming. Coward.

"I accessorized the dragon," Amy corrected. "There wasn't any rescue."

The princess frowned. "But who am I supposed to marry?"

"I bet there are some other princes on their way," Charming said. "You can marry the next one to arrive."

"You will be greatly rewarded," the princess said to Charming. "Would you like a token of my appreciation?"

Charming backed away from her. "No, thank you."

We turned to go, but she ran around us and cut us off. "You can't just leave me here. The dragon could return."

"So don't stay here," Edgar said.

"You could just have her kiss you and break the spell," I whispered to Charming.

Charming shook his head. "No way. I'd rather be a rat than risk getting stuck in Happily Ever After with her."

My respect for Charming grew a little bit in that moment, but when you're starting at zero, a little was a lot.

Lady Laurel appeared next to the princess. "Amaryllis, you are not supposed to have that wand. You're grounded." She put her hand on Amy's shoulder, and they vanished.

"Hey!" the princess yelled. "Where's my beautiful dress? What kind of fairy godmother are you?"

I sat on a burnt tree stump. How could Lady Laurel take Amy away now? We were just starting to have fun together. I didn't even get a chance to ask if she could get us matching shoes. How long was she going to be grounded? And who was going to get rid of my frogs and slugs? I'd already been nice most of the day. I couldn't go much longer without insulting someone.

Horses thundered down the path, kicking up a cloud of dust. "Your ride is here," I said to the princess. The Quest was no fun without Amy. I just wanted to go home.

The princess studied us for a moment. Her eyes rested on Edgar a little longer than anyone else, or rather on his shirt. She mouthed our last name—Perilous. Then she screamed, threw her hands up in the air, and ran to the horsemen.

"What's wrong with her?" I asked.

Charming wiped the blade of his sword with his shirt. "I don't know. Habit?" He inspected the blade and wiped an invisible smudge with his thumb.

"How fare ye, fair maiden?" the knight on the first horse asked. I threw up a little in my mouth.

"The Perilous twins!" the princess cried. "They were going to feed me to their giant rat."

Five very large knights jumped off their very large horses and ran at us with raised swords. "Run!" I yelled, and this time the boys followed me.

# Thirteen

**W**e didn't get past the cave. A giant knight grabbed me by the waist and threw me over his shoulder. Pounding his armored body wouldn't do any good, so I screamed into his helmet. My voice echoed loud enough that it even hurt my head.

"Stop screaming," the knight said, holding me at a distance.

I didn't stop.

"Unhand me, you knave," Charming said. "I am Prince Charming."

The knight holding Charming tied his paws together and tossed him over the back of his horse. I had no problem treating Charming like he was a common rat, but I didn't like seeing anyone else do it.

"I'm a prince too," Edgar said. "Technically. And my sister is a princess. You are going to be sorry when her fairy godmother hears about this."

The knight holding Edgar put a gag over his mouth and tied his hands together.

"We didn't capture the princess. Can't you see she's lying?" I yelled.

The knight threw me over the back of his horse, and we plodded up the path. I struggled to free myself, even if that meant falling off the horse. "Free me!" The knight only paused long enough to shove a dirty sock into my mouth. The horror. I did the only thing I could do. I dropped all pretense of being nice and insulted the knight's horse and mother in one sentence, which was not easy to do with a dirty sock in my mouth. The resulting frog pushed the sock out in its glorious leap for freedom.

I spit out slime and bit the only place that wasn't covered in armor—the knight's knee. My mouth was already full of germs, so what did I have to lose?

"Aaaargh!" The knight pulled his horse to a stop. "Why, you little wench!" He raised his hand to slap me, but fortunately, there was another knight who was paying attention.

"Stop!" The other knight yanked me away and set me on his horse. "Haven't you noticed how perfect her hair is, despite being thrown over the back of a horse?" He clunked the first knight on the head with his gauntlet. "Her brother speaks the truth. She is a princess." He paused to tie my hands together. "An evil princess, but a princess no less. Knights do not strike princesses."

"I'm no less evil than the princess you're supposed to be rescuing," I said. "We rescued her from the dragon. She's lying."

"Didn't see a dragon," my new knight captor said. He clicked his tongue, and his great beast of a horse plodded down the path.

"It flew away in an orange tutu." I pointed my nose in the direction the dragon had gone since my hands were tied up.

"Mmm-hmm."

"There were bones everywhere. Charming is a massive rat, but not that massive. Besides, he's into health food—spinach and other gross stuff."

The knight was quiet for a while. He had to see the reason in the situation. Then he said, "You named your giant rat Charming?"

"No. He's Prince Charming. If you would just let us explain . . ."

The knight's armor creaked. "Why would a dragon wear a tutu?"

"Amy, an untrained fairy godmother, accessorized him."

He paused for a minute. "Didn't see an Amy either. Where did this Amy go?"

"She was taken away by my fairy godmother, Lady Laurel."

"Why should I believe a Perilous? Especially when your brother proudly wears the name on his garment."

"That's his gym shirt. They make us write our names on them. No one wears their gym clothes proudly. We all look like idiots."

He was quiet for a moment. I had a feeling that he knew more about us than he let on.

"I have never heard of a place that makes you wear shirts with your name on them."

"We live in the real world. They're really into labeling there."

"Do you keep many heroes as pets?"

"Charming isn't a pet. He's an accident. We don't have any other pets, unless you count Dad's cockroach. Worst birthday present ever, but I never expect a lot from Grandma Perilous."

"Your Grandma Perilous sent you a cockroach?"

"Yep."

"Single file!" a knight from the front of the group called. The horses fell in line as we approached what appeared to be a massive pile of shoes.

"Are those shoes?" I asked.

"Indeed." A pair of black winged flats zipped over to us, and the knight shooed them away. "The king really needs to do something about his elf problem. They're out of control again."

We turned up a steep slope and my left shoe fell off. The winged flats zipped over, and one slid on my bare foot. It looked like Amy's shoe and was surprisingly comfortable. I kicked my right shoe off, and the other flying shoe replaced it. They fit a lot better than my old shoes. The knight didn't say anything, so he either didn't notice or didn't care. A pair of sneakers popped up from the ground in front of us, startling the horse.

"Easy, girl." The knight patted the horse's neck. "It's just shoes."

"Why are there so many shoes?" I asked. The sneakers slunk over to the nearest mound and dove in. I wished I could follow. There was a pair of long, black boots I really wanted to try on. Amy would probably like this place too.

A brown boot flew from a nearby pile of shoes. The knight ducked just before the thing would have hit his head. "This is where the cobbler elves go when they don't have anyone to help."

Each mound of shoes steadily got shorter the farther we went. Then there were only a few pairs hiding under bushes or romping in the mud. The trees cleared, and the path opened into a wide green meadow with one little man sitting in the middle on a short stump.

"Leprechaun?" I guessed.

"Never ask him about his gold," the knight advised. "He's sensitive."

"Ooookaaaay," I said slowly. "Sir . . ."

"Sir Joe."

The leprechaun glared at us until we left the meadow. The sun beat on the back of our necks. I regretted wearing black. "That suit of armor must be like wearing an oven," I said.

"Umph."

I was not used to riding massive horse beasts. My legs cramped.

"Stop wiggling," Sir Joe said.

"It's uncomfortable," I complained. "Are we almost there?"

"Soon."

One of the knights ahead shouted. Something dropped from his horse and scurried away into the forest. "The rat got away!"

Charming and I had been separated by three horses for hours. Apparently, it was far enough for him to turn back into a rat. I should have been relieved to be free of him, but something in my chest constricted. Charming wasn't used to being a rat. How would he survive? I watched the back of Edgar's head. We were down to two members of our group.

Smoke curled up from Edgar's hands. As soon as he'd burned through his ties, he vaulted off the horse and vanished in the trees.

I was alone with five overheated knights and a loathsome princess. Ew.

# Fourteen

"They abandoned you." Sir Joe informed me as his companions searched for Charming and my brother.

"It was horrible," the loathsome princess said. She sniffed and wiped her nose on her sleeve.

"Not as horrible as using your clothes as a tissue," I said.

She glared at me. "I think almost getting eaten by a dragon—I mean, a giant rat—is the worst thing ever."

"What did you say?" Sir Joe asked.

My stomach unknotted just a little. "She said—" But I never got to finish my sentence because she fainted—or at least pretended to faint. And that's when it occurred to me that I wasn't nearly as evil as this princess. I had a sudden urge to say something nice, just to prove that I wasn't like her. "Thank you for stopping that other knight from hitting me, Sir Joe."

Something pulsed just under my heart. I coughed and choked out a ruby. It glinted in my hand. I'd said nice things before, but I'd never had jewels fall from my lips. What was going on here?

Gauntleted hands took my elbow. The leader of the knights snatched the ruby from my hand, and it vanished inside his glove. Joe had been too busy helping the loathsome princess to see anything. "I'd better keep the Perilous girl with me, Joe. Why don't you go help search for her brother and the rat?"

The other knights returned empty-handed, their armor creaking as they shook their heads. Telling them about the ruby wouldn't do me any good. They'd probably stick another sock in my mouth.

"I think the others gave up, Sir Rodney. I can keep the Perilous girl." Joe's eyes squinted inside his helmet. I hoped the sun wasn't frying his brain inside that metal bucket. He seemed to be the only decent knight of the bunch.

The loathsome princess had a sudden recovery and sat up straight. "But, Rodney, *I* was riding with you." She stuck out her lower lip. Having my hands tied and being held captive by a giant knight were the only things that stopped me from slugging her.

Rodney set me on his horse. "I need to be sure she doesn't escape before I secure your hand in marriage."

The loathsome princess stared into his eyes, no doubt trying to figure out if he was handsome. Anyone who went around with a bucket on their head all day couldn't possibly be handsome, especially in this heat. Half-baked, yes, but never handsome.

The castle came into view after another hour of traveling. "You guys need to get a car," I complained. "Even a bus would be better than this." I wriggled my bottom, willing the blood to return to my legs.

"Do not speak, foul witch," Rodney said.

I slouched to take up as much room as possible. He should know all about foul witches. He was about to marry one. I couldn't think of two people who deserved each other more.

People dressed in homespun clothes emerged from tiny huts. A few ventured toward us and tilted their dirty faces in our direction. Rodney didn't slow.

"They rescued two princesses," an elderly man said. He smiled at me, showing off his toothless gums. "This one's even prettier than the first."

The loathsome princess gasped. I grinned. Being called pretty was okay as long as it bothered her. "Thank you, kind sir." A golden coin fell out of my mouth, and he scrambled to retrieve it.

"Shut up," Rodney growled.

I covered my mouth with my hands. Where had that come from?

"We have captured one of the vicious Perilous twins," Rodney announced. He yanked my hair.

"Ouch!" I swatted at his hand and, unfortunately, hit his metal glove. People in the crowd were muttering my last name. "We aren't from around here," I said. Why did they all look so terrified?

"She's too cute to be a Perilous," someone yelled.

"Her brother escaped," Rodney announced. "He wears a shirt that bears the name Perilous."

The crowd gasped. A child pelted me with a rotten turnip. What kind of kid carries a rotten turnip around with them?

"Your mother needs to teach you some manners, urchin," I said. "You're the kind of kid that gets carried off by trolls." It was true. The naughty ones always got carried off by monsters. Although sometime the nice ones did too. Come to think of it, just being a kid made them eligible to be carried off by trolls.

"We shall keep her locked up in the castle. I do hope the village doesn't suffer too many losses due to her brother and their giant man-eating rat."

The village people vanished inside their pathetic huts with their rotten turnips and locked their doors. Even the old man that got the gold coin was gone.

The castle was a somber, gray stone building of epic proportions. A hunched-back man cranked a wheel on the far side of the moat, lowering the drawbridge.

The kids back home were probably eating lunch and wondering where we were. What would the cheerleaders giggle about without Edgar and Charming? The horse's hooves clomped on the wooden drawbridge, startling a school of goldfish.

"Goldfish?" I asked.

"Shut up!" Rodney hissed.

"Someone woke up on the wrong side of the horse today," I muttered.

A flock of young boys came running from the stables. Actually, I didn't know for sure they were coming from the stables, other than the fact that they smelled like they came straight from the stables.

"Hello, pretty princess," one of the boys said to me.

"You saved the wrong princess," another boy pointed out. "But I like this one better. Can we keep her?"

I smiled, and the loathsome princess gasped again. "I'm here, you idiot," she said between her teeth.

"Maybe the dragon will come back for her," the boy said.

"Rat," Rodney corrected.

"The princess doesn't like to be called a rat," the boy whispered to Rodney.

"She's not a rat," Rodney roared. "I meant the dragon."

"The dragon isn't a rat." The boy scratched his filthy head with his even filthier hands. "He had big green wings and breathed fire."

Rodney jumped off his horse and dragged me with him. "The princess was kidnapped by this girl's rat."

The boy winked at me. "Sure. Whatever you say."

The king and queen marched out of the castle, followed by a woman whose face was obscured by a dark cloak. The stable boys made a wide path so they could get through them. "We would like to thank the noble knight who rescued the princess and offer her hand in marriage," the queen said.

"Who's the lucky knight?" the king asked.

All the knights quickly pointed to Rodney.

Rodney bowed to the king and queen. "I rescued her from this." He pointed at me. I opened my mouth to defend myself. The cloaked woman waved her hand, and my tongue froze.

Rodney pushed me to another knight. Knights, like cheerleaders, all looked the same in uniform. I could only hope that he'd shoved me in the direction of Sir Joe. "Lock her in the dungeon while we make the arrangements." The knight nodded, and the royal party returned to the castle with the loathsome princess. My mouth went back to normal the moment the cloaked woman left.

Rodney removed his helmet, revealing a sad little fringe of red hair that didn't quite make it to the top of his head. All he needed was white face paint and a red nose.

I snorted before realizing what he'd said. "Wait. Did you say lock her up in the *dungeon*?"

# Fifteen

Dungeon? He couldn't be serious. I'd spent my life preparing for a tower. "Princesses don't get locked in dungeons," I explained. "They're way too dirty. I demand to talk to . . ." My parents were out of cell phone range, my brother had deserted me, Charming was a rat, the knights in shining armor hated me (although in fairness the feeling was mutual), and my fairy godmother was the one who had sent me to this hideous place. There wasn't anyone to talk to. "I don't suppose you have any lawyers around here, do you?"

The knight holding me removed his helmet. He was dad-verging-on-grandfather-age and had so much graying brown hair that it was hard to determine where the hair on his head ended and his beard began. "It's Joe," he whispered.

I raised an eyebrow and let him continue.

"I believe you." Then he started toward the castle with me in tow.

"Wait," I said, dragging my heels. "Where are we going?"

"To the dungeon. I have to follow orders."

I wrapped my arms around a wooden post. "But I'm innocent. You said so yourself."

Joe unwrapped my arms from the post and dragged me out into the open. "True, but you're also a Perilous. The dungeon is the safest place for you while I look into things."

"Dungeons aren't safe. They're full of torture chambers and skeletons chained to walls."

Joe took me through the courtyard, past the throngs of vile-smelling peasants, and into the castle. You would think with the amount of magic around, they would be able to come up with some soap or an air freshener. We went down stairs that spiraled into darkness. It took forever to get down all those stairs, but that might have been because I was trying to go up while Joe insisted on going down.

Joe put me in a dark cell with a dirty straw mat and a bucket in the corner. It smelled like scurvy. "I can't stay here," I yelled through the metal bars of the cell door. "It's full of disease. I'm too young to die by flea infestation."

"I'll send someone down with a bucket and a mop." He stepped out of my view for a minute and then reappeared with three small cages. "I almost forgot. The cell comes with a complimentary rat friend."

"Ew." I stepped back.

"Come on, pick one." He held them up and showed off his brown teeth in what was probably supposed to be a smile. "It's part of the dungeon experience."

"I don't want the dungeon experience." I was about to tell him where he could stick those rats, despite the guaranteed delivery of a frog, when I noticed a small brown spot, slightly to the left, on the nose of the middle one. It had to be Charming. I pointed to the rat in the cage next to him. "That one looks like it wants to eat me."

Joe sighed. "Rats are really very friendly." He put the offending rat down. There were two left. "You aren't afraid of your giant rat."

"He isn't my giant rat. He's Prince Charming. And he's under an unfortunate spell."

"He looked like a rat to me when he scurried off into the woods. Fast little guy, but we'll find him." He held up the two cages, and I managed to keep my expression somber as he held up the very rat that he was looking for.

"That one looks dirty," I said, pointing to the other rat that wasn't Charming. "I bet it's carrying a plague."

Joe shoved Charming's cage in my cell and slammed the door. "This one it is. Don't forget to feed him. You can expect some gruel in an hour or so."

I waited for Joe to clear out and then rushed to Charming. He scurried out as soon as I had the latch unlocked.

"Charming?" I whispered, suddenly nervous. Rats really do carry the plague. Images of me languishing in a cell with pus-filled blisters filled my mind. "Is that you?"

The rat twitched his whiskers, ran over a wooden slat covering the bottom of the cell door, and disappeared between the metal bars.

"Charming?"

His little claws scratched the stone floor until he was well out of my sight.

"I didn't want a rat friend anyway," I informed the bare stone walls. Although, it wasn't really empty. It was full of germs. I couldn't move for fear of kicking them up into the air. I was sure I'd be dead within an hour. At least I wouldn't have to be subjected to prison gruel.

Moisture welled up in my eyes, and a single tear rolled down my cheek. It landed on the ground with a clatter.

Diamond tears. Perfect. Mom never mentioned diamond tears. Then again, she had probably never cried a day in her life. I've never met anyone so chronically happy. Something in this crazy world had switched me from slimy creatures to jewels. It wasn't anything I did. I hadn't changed, not really. I'd said nice things before and wasn't inundated with jewels.

Something in the hall clunked, and then metal scraped across the stone floor. I looked between the bars in the door, careful not to touch the filthy things, but I couldn't see anything in the gloom. Only a small trickle of light could get through the filthy window.

The scraping continued in short spurts. It was getting closer.

"Hello?" I called. The empty dungeon echoed my greeting and mixed it with the scraping sound.

A small white creature lurched toward me. I was about to scream, when I realized it was Charming. At least, I was pretty sure it was Charming. He had a key ring that was twice the size of his body clenched in his teeth. The key scraped the ground as he scurried toward me.

"Charming?"

He flicked his tail at me and dropped the key ring. He narrowed a beady eye and studied my cell door.

"I guess rat friends only get to speak in magical towers." Not that I was counting him as a friend. Assistant would be a more appropriate word, or minion. I'd always wanted a minion.

He squeaked and went back to studying the door. The wooden slat along the bottom of the door was no doubt put there so a rat friend couldn't help the prisoner escape. Charming didn't have any problem scurrying over it alone, but there was no way he could get that massive key ring over the plate. It was also too high for me to reach down and get it.

"Now what?"

Charming shrugged. Worst. Minion. Ever.

I took inventory. I had a cell phone with no service, a rat, a magic carabiner for escaping towers, and an empty stomach. The window was too small for even me to squeeze through. The only way out was the door, and I had to get the key before I could go that way. I unclipped the carabiner and lowered it to Charming with the magic line. "Hook that to the key, and I'll pull it up."

He hooked my carabiner to the key ring, and the line in my hand automatically shortened. I took a deep breath before reaching through the filthy bars to get the key. My hand fit through, but I had to actually touch the bars in order to get the key in the lock.

Charming squeaked at me.

"Don't rush me."

Charming stood on his hind legs and made twisting motions with his front paws.

"Not helping." I bit my lip. Once we escaped, I could find a nice stream and wash away the germs, or I could get Edgar to zap them with his magic. Then I would slug him for abandoning me. I stretched my arm through the bars and twisted my wrist toward the lock. I fit the key inside, and it easily turned. The door swung open.

Charming and I stared at the door. "That was easy," I said. I wrapped the carabiner around my wrist. My clothes were changed too often for me to ever trust a pocket or belt loop with it again.

Charming squeaked.

I had the feeling he thought it was too easy. I agreed. "Now what?"

He stood up on his hind legs and slashed his paws back and forth. I couldn't help but smile. A rat pretending to sword fight was the most adorable thing I'd seen all day. It was also the most ridiculous plan I'd ever heard.

"Fighting our way out sounds fun, but I think it would be better to sneak out. I'm not much of a fighter."

Charming shook his head and pointed at himself before making the slashing motions again.

"It's nice that you want to fight, but you're just a cute little rat." I patted his head.

He shook his head again and took a heroic pose, like the ones where the hero is standing with one foot on a rock with his sword lifted high. It was so cute, I almost sighed before I remembered myself.

He pointed to his empty sword paw.

"Are you hurt?" The key was a little sharp.

He shook his head and pointed to his empty paw again.

"You want to use the key as a weapon?"

He shook his head and looked around, like he was missing something.

"You miss your sword?"

He nodded.

"But you're too small to carry a sword. I don't think they make them in your size."

He did something with his tail that didn't look polite at all.

"You want your sword back, then?"

Charming nodded and rushed to the stairs. I followed him into the darkness, keeping my hand on the wall for balance.

"Those knights probably still have your sword." We went up a lot of stairs, my footsteps echoing around us, before I stopped to catch my breath. Both shoes were still on my feet. Not only did they match my almost-BFF's shoes, but they also somehow didn't fall off every third step.

A tiny window far above our heads let in a trickle of light. We weren't moving, but footsteps were still echoing in the stairwell. "We aren't alone, Charming."

His little ears swiveled up and down. Finally, he pointed down the steps.

"Are you sure?" I whispered. "No one was down there with us."

Charming scurried to the step below me, which meant he was either still trying to protect me, or the footsteps were actually coming from above.

I pushed my back into the wall and tried to make myself as small as possible. A gentle glow appeared below us. Beady red eyes peered at me. I screamed, just a little, and then realized it was just Charming.

"Raven, is that you?" Amy appeared in all her sparkly glory and put her hand over her heart. "That was a lot of stairs."

"How did you get down there?" I asked.

She held up a new wand. "I borrowed Lady Laurel's new wand. It wasn't supposed to arrive until tomorrow."

Charming scurried up the step and hid behind my leg. The coward. I, on the other hand, was impressed by her klepto skills. It takes a special kind of person to steal a wand from a fairy godmother. Amy was proving to be more evil than meets the eye.

"I thought you were locked up, so I came to get you out. I guess you figured it out by yourself."

I thought about clueing her in on Charming, but I figured I owed him one for dragging the key to me. Her magic kind of scared me too. "Dungeons aren't my thing, so I left." Charming climbed up the back of my pants, which tickled. I held my foot out for her to see. "Look at these cute shoes I found along the way."

"Ooh, those are super cute. They're like mine without the sparkle."

"I know. And the best part is that they don't fall off my feet."

Amy fingered the flower jewel pinned to her shirt. "I doubt there's anything about those old shoes that you'll miss. I like your new ones much better." She cocked her head to the side and gave me a tiny smile. "I can help you get up the stairs."

My mouth went dry. "Oh, you don't have to . . ."

"Of course I do, but I can't stick around. Lady Laurel will notice that I'm gone." Red sparks erupted from the end of her wand and surrounded me. The stairs disappeared, and I found myself standing on a tower roof. She'd helped me up the stairs all right.

# Sixteen

The castle and village were surrounded by green forest on all sides. The green abruptly ended with white to the east of us. Another castle stood in the distance, white as the snow that surrounded it. The knights were camped behind the castle below me on the south side. I had no idea which way home was, but I decided to avoid the Winterland, the front of the castle, and the knights, which left us with one direction—west.

"Charming," I whispered even though no one was around. Whispering seemed appropriate since we were escaping from prison. "Hang on to my shirt. I'm going to rappel off this tower to the castle wall below us. We're going to have to climb down on the west side so no one can see us."

Charming craned his furry little neck over the side and then made slashing motions with his paw.

I sighed. "I know you want your sword. We'll have to sneak back around the castle, but I'm not going to get it. You'll have to drag it out of there somehow."

He nodded. I was hoping that he'd see reason and stop

trying to get us caught over a hunk of metal. Apparently, nothing can come between a boy and his sword.

I wrapped my magic carabiner line around a flagpole. Charming scurried up to my shoulder, and I climbed to the edge. A horn blared somewhere below us and footsteps thundered up the steps. Crap. Someone had discovered that we were missing. I lowered us off the side of the tower and rappelled to the main castle roof. The carabiner quietly returned to my hand. I huddled next to the wall, out of sight from the ground and the tower above.

"I don't see anyone!" a rough voice yelled above us.

"Me neither, but we can't stop searching. That old witch is as crazy as she is ugly. I don't think my wife would let me in the house if I was turned into a toad."

Charming squeaked in my ear.

"There was a witch with the king and queen," I whispered. "I don't think she likes me." Charming made a squeak that sounded suspiciously like a snort.

We kept to the shadows as I tiptoed across the roof. My heart pounded with every step. Eventually, one of the searchers had to check the roof. Something crunched under my feet. I froze. Surely someone inside heard that. There was no sound except for the wind blowing in Winterland. I shivered.

We dropped down to the ground and crept around the castle, ducking behind every bush and chubby tree. The knights' camp was abandoned, except for Rodney and the witch. Charming's sword was strapped to Rodney's horse.

"You said she only held value for you," Rodney said.

"She does, unless you value frogs and slugs."

Rodney held up what could only be the ruby I'd spewed

on the way to the castle. I hoped it had some rather nasty germs on it from my mouth. "What's this, then?"

"A ruby. She must have been carrying it. Tell your men to look for frogs. If you find the frogs, you'll find the girl. She must be absolutely furious by now. They should be pouring out of her mouth like water."

"I think she's more valuable than you're letting on. I want my pay doubled."

The old woman leaned forward, her face still concealed under the hood. "How would you like to be the lead frog in our hunt?"

Rodney shook his head and pocketed the ruby. "You're right. She must have been carrying it."

Another knight ran across the field carrying a stack of cages. Inside each cage was a rat. "We found more rats."

"Good. Put them with the other ones."

The knight vanished from my sight for a moment as he set the rats somewhere around the corner from us. Charming shuddered. The old woman raised her arms, and her long sleeves slipped down far enough to reveal the end of a wand. She waved her arms in a wide circle, chanting something under her breath. The air crackled, and the rat on my shoulder suddenly got very heavy. I fell over backward with Charming sitting on my chest.

He scurried off my chest, still a rat, only bigger.

"She made you look less human than Amy did."

"Quiet," Charming hissed. He covered my mouth with his paw.

I nodded, and we tiptoed into the woods. It was hard enough getting around the castle with just me and a rat-sized Charming. Someone was sure to notice a Charming-sized rat. "I think we're safe." Naturally, that was when my phone rang. I dug into my pocket to shut it up.

"I thought you were out of range," Charming whispered.

"I thought so too!"

"What's that sound?" Rodney asked.

"Shut it up!" Charming hissed.

I dug the thing out of my pocket and hit ignore, since turning it off would take too long and came with a loud chime. We hurried into the trees, stepping as quietly as possible. Armor flashed in the woods behind us.

"I see the giant rat!"

"Get it!"

"Let's split up," Charming said. "They're after me."

"That sounds like a stupid idea," I said. Surprisingly no frogs appeared. "They want both of us."

Charming suddenly grabbed me and jumped. We soared to a high branch. Apparently, being a rat had its perks. We held very still as the knights ran under our tree and disappeared into the woods.

"Now what?" I mouthed.

Another knight came down the path and stopped under us. He walked a little distance and then paused. My phone rang again. The knight craned his metal head up in our direction and laughter echoed from his helmet. He removed the helmet. It was Joe.

Joe held his finger up to his mouth. I hit the ignore button on my phone. Then Joe walked away. My phone rang again. This time I answered it. Someone was about to get a lecture on crappy timing.

"Hello?"

"Raven! It's Edgar."

"How did you get the phone to work?" Charming asked.

Edgar must have heard him. "I'm using magic to establish a connection between our phones. Where are you?"

"I'm sitting in a tree with a giant rat while foul knights in shining armor hunt for me."

"Oh good, you're safe. You know that app Dad made so we could always find each other?" I tapped the screen and activated the app just as I heard him say, "Don't use it." Charming grabbed my hand and the trees vanished, only to be replaced with metal bars. We were in another dungeon.

# Seventeen

Edgar put his phone down and shook his head at me. "Which part of 'don't use it' did you not understand?"

"The part where you didn't say it fast enough," I said.

The dungeon was cleaner than the one I had come from. Everything was white, including the small bench in the corner that Edgar was sitting on. It was also freezing. Poor Edgar's lips were blue since he was still in his gym clothes.

I sat next to him and elbowed him. "This is better than the last dungeon I escaped from. It had mean knights and an evil witch."

Edgar raised an eyebrow. "Evil witch?"

I shrugged. "You didn't think we could go through the Enchanted Forest without meeting an evil witch, did you?" I looked around. "Where are we anyway?"

Edgar ran his fingers over his mouth and mumbled something that sounded like "tooth fairies."

Charming laughed. "I swear you just said, 'tooth fairies.'"

"Mm-hmm." Edgar pointed at the wall. "Take a closer

look." I leaned closer to the wall and jumped back. It was made out of billions of old baby teeth. "Lady Laurel wasn't kidding when she said the tooth fairy was impressed with my teeth cleaning spell. What she failed to mention was that there is actually an army of tooth fairies who are tired of keeping their castle sparkly white. Tooth fairies aren't as cute and sweet as you'd think."

"Sweets are bad for your teeth," a perky little voice said. A tiny fairy dressed in miniature scrubs flew into the dungeon.

"How were you hiding in the dark?" I asked. "I thought fairies glowed."

The fairy's laughter reminded me of icicles falling off trees and shattering on the sidewalk below. "How would we collect teeth from under kids' pillows if we glowed? Fairies don't glow." She wiped a bitty tear from her eye. "You would not believe the nonsense people believe when it comes to fairies. Clap your hands, indeed."

I looked at Charming for help. "Amy glows."

"Who's Amy?" the tooth fairy asked.

"She's a fairy godmother in training."

"Fairy godmothers aren't fairies. They're just nice witches, and they don't glow either. Only bewitched people glow."

"Bewitched?"

"Of course. She's under a spell. Magic surrounds her, but she isn't in control of it," the fairy said.

"We already knew that," Charming said. He scratched his furry ear.

I knew Amy wasn't being completely honest with me, but she was my friend. We even had matching shoes. "I thought . . ."

The fairy cut me off. "That's the problem. Too many people thinking. You're better off here, cleaning teeth." She turned to Edgar. "Your break is over. Time to get to work. I have no idea where your friends came from, and I don't care. They mean less work for me." She dug two full-sized toothbrushes from a pocket half their size and handed them to Charming and me. "Brand-new toothbrushes!" Her wings buzzed as she zipped between the prison bars. The door opened behind her.

"I don't clean," I said. It was the only perk of being a princess. Mom has the house set on self-clean. I didn't even make my bed.

The fairy flitted back to us. "You will now," she said, her voice sickly sweet.

I closed my eyes and took a deep breath. No fairy was going to make me scrub old dead teeth. I opened my eyes wide and struck an adorable pose. "Please?" A diamond fell from my lips and clattered to the floor.

The fairy clasped her hands and sighed. "Ah, aren't you cute?" She turned to the boys. "Isn't she cute?"

Edgar closed his eyes. "Meh."

"I think you'll look even cuter scrubbing teeth," the fairy said as she flitted down the hall.

"What?" How could my cuteness not have worked?

"Scrubby, scrubby," a tiny voice echoed from the hall.

I thought about kicking the wall but didn't because it would ruin my new shoes. I hate my life.

"What's stopping us from escaping?" Charming whispered.

Edgar pointed to his gym clothes. "I'll freeze to death out there."

"If we could contact Amy, she could accessorize you," I said.

"No way." Charming shook his head. "She's an imposter. You heard what the fairy said. She's bewitched."

"But she'd never hurt us. Maybe the tooth fairy is wrong. Maybe she isn't bewitched. Her personality is pretty sparkly. Even you thought she was a fairy, or something, when we first met, Charming."

Charming shrugged. "How would I know anything about fairies? I studied sword fighting, not sparkles. And that was before she pick-pocketed your fairy godmother."

Edgar stepped between us. "Amy has been living in the Enchanted Forest all this time, Raven. I don't think she's really your friend."

"I think she is." We liked the same shoes. She had to be my friend. "She did lie to me, but she's also our best chance to get back home."

"All I know is that she was the one with wand in hand when I turned into a rat," Charming said.

"I thought you were blaming me."

"You are a Perilous. Blaming you was natural."

Edgar stooped over and grabbed the diamond. "Since when did you start producing jewels?"

"Since today." I ran my fingers through my hair. "This place is getting to me. I want to go home."

"Unfortunately, that's not an option at the moment," Edgar said. "Those tooth fairies can get ugly if you don't do what they say."

I decided it was better to believe him than to attempt mutiny on my own, for now.

Edgar led the way out of the dungeon, up a flight of stairs, and through a maze of tooth-covered hallways. "This is where I've been working."

The hallway was lined with little yellow teeth. I

swallowed hard. This place was a nightmare. "I am not touching those little germ havens."

"You don't have to touch them. The toothbrush does all the touching." The little tooth fairy appeared out of nowhere. Apparently, we weren't as free to escape as I'd hoped. "This way." She prodded me in the direction of some especially yellow teeth as Charming whipped out his toothbrush and Edgar waved his arms.

The tooth fairy led me down the hall and past some ornate doors covered in gold-filled teeth. "What's in there?"

"That's the molar room." The fairy sighed. "The tooth fairy queen has a special group of servants to keep those teeth clean. We get precious few molars since most kids stop believing in us by the time they lose them." She flitted past a window lined with a thick curtain and pointed at a wall. "Brushy, brushy!"

The curtain gave me an idea. As soon as she was out of sight, I set my phone on vibrate and slid it behind the curtain. Then I took a deep breath and brandished my new toothbrush. Suds appeared from the bristles, and the brush vibrated as soon as I held it to the wall. It was a shame to waste a magic toothbrush on a stupid wall. The air around me went from smelling like stale breath to peppermint. I glanced nonchalantly at the window. My phone was well hidden behind the curtains.

Charming and Edgar whispered to each other down the hall. Edgar pointed at me, and Charming slowly turned.

"What?" I said.

"You *are* more adorable when scrubbing yellow teeth," Charming declared.

I hate my life.

The tooth fairy came back for us after hours of

mind-numbing scrubbing. Every attempt I'd made to explore the castle was met with a grumpy tooth fairy leading me back to my spot and singing "scrubby, scrubby." They were a lot more vigilant than they let on. I bet they flossed twice a day too.

My arms ached as she led us back down to the dungeon. "Let me get that for you." The door opened without anyone touching it and then slammed behind us.

"Thanks a lot," I said. A big lump formed over my tongue. The fairy watched me fish it out of my mouth with interest—until she saw what it was.

"Too bad," she said. "It's just an emerald."

"Just an emerald?"

"We only value baby teeth." She squinted at my mouth, which I promptly shut tight. "I don't suppose you have any left? You've probably lost them already."

I actually did have a few baby teeth left, but I wasn't about to tell her. "Why are you keeping us locked up like this? What did we do?"

"You came to us."

"I didn't come to you," Edgar said.

"We kidnapped you. Well, I kidnapped you." She puffed up her tiny chest. "Your spell does not disappoint. The hall of front teeth has never been so shiny."

I vowed then and there that if I ever had children, I would never tell them to leave their teeth under their pillow. If they were desperate for money, I'd hand them a quarter. "How did you find out about his spell?"

"An old witch told us." I was pretty sure I knew which witch she was talking about, but I didn't understand why. What would an old witch have against us, and how did she know about Edgar's spell? The fairy snapped her fingers, and a tray of food appeared. And by food, I mean nothing edible. It was full of vegetables. She flew away, leaving a fresh minty scent behind her.

My stomach grumbled. "I'm starving, and they bring us rabbit food?"

"It looks delicious." Charming attacked a stalk of celery with the ferocity of a rat.

I nibbled on a carrot stick. It was better than nothing, but not a lot. My only hope for a real meal was to escape. The fairy was gone so I figured it was safe to share my secret. I leaned forward and whispered, "I left my phone upstairs behind some curtains. We can use the find-each-other app, pop upstairs, use the curtains as blankets, and make a run for it."

"Not a bad plan, for a girl," Edgar whispered. "Link arms with me." Charming and I stood on either side of Edgar and linked our arms around his. Edgar activated the find-each-other app on his phone. The cell disappeared around us, and we found ourselves . . . in another cell down the hall. My phone was in the middle of the floor with a few extra toothbrushes.

"This cell is smaller," Charming said, rolling his eyes.

I picked my phone up from the floor and desperately clicked on the go home button. It didn't even light up.

"Nice try," the fairy said, appearing behind us.

"If you expect us to keep working, you could at least provide us with some real food," I said. My stomach grumbled.

The fairy floated another food tray into our cell. It was spinach leaves. I handed it to Charming.

"There must be some way you'll let us go," I said.

"I already told you, the only thing we value is baby teeth."

Edgar pointed to a baby tooth he should have had

pulled years ago. It already had the adult tooth behind it. "You can have this one. It's not really loose, though."

The tooth fairy flitted over to him. "Too bad it isn't a molar." She seemed to consider for a moment, and then she said, "Open up."

Edgar opened his mouth. I took his hand in case he needed comfort. The fairy reached for the tooth, and Edgar squeezed my hand so hard I thought it would break. The fairy gave one solid yank and held his bloody tooth up in the air. "Doesn't get fresher than that."

Ew. "Can we go now?" I asked.

"That was only one baby tooth. Edgar doesn't have any more." She turned to us.

"I lost all my baby teeth already," Charming said.

"I wouldn't take yours anyway." She turned to me and raised a tiny brow.

Only one of my molars was loose. I bit my lip and took a deep breath. "I have a loose baby molar."

The tooth fairy gasped.

"But if I give it to you, you have to return us to the forest where you kidnapped Edgar."

The tooth fairy's fingers twitched. She looked around. "It's a deal."

The tooth was pretty loose. I opened my mouth and closed my eyes. The tooth fairy yanked the tooth out before I could take a breath. My mouth filled with blood. It was even worse than frogs.

"That's two teeth. I will send two of you back to the forest."

"But that wasn't our deal!" I yelled. I pulled a tissue from my pocket and crammed it in my mouth to soak up the blood.

"I agreed to return you to the forest. We never agreed how many of you would be returned. There is another molar in there," she said, her eyes sparkling with greed.

"But I gave you a molar! The other one isn't loose."

The fairy cracked her knuckles. "Someone has to provide for the rat."

"No!" Charming yelled. "I can't ask you to do that. I'll stay here and scrub walls."

Saving Charming against his will held certain appeal. "If I let you take the tooth, you'll return all three of us to the forest where you got Edgar?"

She nodded, her tiny body quivering with excitement.

"In a secluded area where no one will see us," Edgar added.

"Fine, fine." The fairy zipped over to my mouth.

"No," Charming said. "You are not going to do this."

I opened my mouth, and the tooth fairy grabbed my tooth. Pain shot through my jaw, and the world turned black.

# Eighteen

When I came to, I was in a tree with two crisp one-dollar bills in my hand. It was still light out. This had to be the longest day in the history of ever. I looked for my phone, but it wasn't in my pocket. It was probably still in that tiny cell with the tooth fairy. I could hear music and cheering in the distance, so I knew I wasn't too deep in the woods. It also meant I was close to another dungeon. I wanted to go back to sleep. The tree wasn't that bad.

"Raven," someone whispered below me.

I peered over my branch and found Edgar and Charming looking up at me.

"Are you all right?" Edgar asked.

I groaned.

"We're back at the castle," Charming whispered. "They're having the wedding. It's my chance to get my sword back."

They were having the wedding already? The bride and groom hadn't even known each other for twenty-four hours. "Fine. Let's get your stupid sword and get out of here."

"It's not stupid."

I climbed down the tree. "It's a sword." My stomach growled. "And I'm starving."

"Hi, Starving," Edgar said.

"Why did you give me that salad if you were hungry?" Charming asked.

"Because spinach is not food. Could we please find something to eat before we do something stupid like risk our lives for a hunk of metal?"

"Would you please stop using the words *stupid* and *sword* together in the same sentence?" Charming asked.

"I said hunk of metal. Not sword."

Edgar stepped between us. "Children."

"I'm older than you," I hissed.

"By thirteen minutes."

"I was born at least fourteen years before both of you," Charming said.

"Those fourteen years do not count," I said.

"Stop it!" Edgar said. "I can't believe you two are turning me into a peacemaker." He shuddered. "It goes against my nature."

"You aren't doing a great job," I said. "I'm not feeling peaceful."

"At least I have that." He didn't look relieved. "Let's go down to the castle once it gets dark. I'll snag some clothes since no one will recognize me. Then we can snag Charming's sword and find some food before your grumbling stomach gives us away."

"What if we hit a *snag*?" I asked.

Charming snorted.

"It'll be hours before it gets dark," I said. "Time seems to be holding still. I'm hungry now, and now will never end."

"The people are busy celebrating," Charming said. "I doubt they'll notice us. Besides, how long do you think we can all sit here quietly and not kill each other?" An especially untalented flute player took up a melody. "Especially if that's what we have to listen to."

"Fine." Edgar covered his ears. "We'll go now. Just stay hidden." Edgar crept toward the castle. Charming and I followed. The flute gave a sudden toot and fell silent.

Several carts were parked around the castle, and a man playing a small stringed instrument was singing about true love. It was almost as nauseating as Edgar becoming a peacemaker, but it was at least better than the untalented flute player. Judging by the amount of tomatoes and rotten turnips splattered everywhere, the people agreed with me.

I followed my nose to a pastry cart.

Charming sniffed, his whiskers twitching. "These smell . . ." He sniffed again.

"Delicious," I said. My mouth watered.

"No." Charming peeked around the cart. "They smell familiar."

I grabbed the back of his shirt. "What are you doing? You can't go out there. People would notice a giant rat. It's not like the real world where people don't notice magic."

His shoulders slumped. "You're right."

"We just need to find you a nice princess. I'm sure we could find one who will kiss you with no strings attached."

"You know," Edgar said, "if you'd just kissed him back home, we wouldn't even be stuck here."

I cringed. He was right. It was an easy way home, and Charming wasn't as disgusting as most boys our age. "Fine. I'll kiss him and get it over with."

"You don't have to do that," Charming said.

My mouth throbbed where the tooth fairy had pulled the second tooth. She was freakishly strong for one so small. I took a deep breath. "I might as well kiss you now, while my mouth is numb from the pain." I quickly leaned forward and planted a kiss on his cheek. Nothing happened.

Edgar rolled his eyes. "You're supposed to kiss him on the lips."

"No lips," Charming and I said together.

I stood and reached into the cart. Charming grabbed my arm. "What are you doing?"

"Getting some food." My stomach growled.

"But that's stealing. This cart belongs to a baker, not the king."

I sighed and then took a deep breath. He was right, as much as I hated to admit it. Fortunately, I had a way to make it right. "I'm sorry I said your sword was stupid." A lump formed on my tongue.

"I'm still not going to let you take stuff from the cart."

I coughed and spit out a gold coin. "Will this be enough to pay for three pastries?"

"Oh," he said, and his ear twitched. "It's enough to buy the entire cart."

"Good. I'll take two pastries then. One for me and one for Edgar." I smirked and tossed the coin inside the cart.

"Ouch," someone muttered. A head popped up from inside the cart. "That hurt."

He had one of those faces that looked familiar, but there was no way I could know him. I hadn't even been in the Enchanted Forest for an entire day. He was kind of cute, in a way-too-old-for-me kind of way, except for the bright red spot on his forehead. Gold coins are heavier than they look.

Edgar and Charming stepped back and hid in the shadows. The guy stared at me. I cleared my throat. "Are you the muffin man? Of course you're the muffin man. You're in the muffin cart. I'd like a muffin."

He rubbed his forehead. "Do you usually pay for your food by assaulting the merchant?"

Charming gasped. "No, it couldn't be."

I shook my head and shoved Charming behind a bush. He was going to get us caught. "That was an accident. I've heard of you. Don't you live on Drury Lane?"

"Of course," he said.

I'd always pictured the muffin man as plump and jolly. This guy was trim and grumpy. Of course, I did just bean him in the head with a gold coin. That might have put a damper on his mood.

"I've always lived on Drury Lane, but I will not die there," he said.

"Umm." Well, that was awkward. "So how about a pastry?"

"You don't have to die on Drury Lane," Charming said.

"Shut up, Charming," I hissed between my teeth. I turned on my best smile and struck a cute pose for the muffin man. It hadn't worked for the tooth fairy, but no man could resist the cuteness of a princess. "Do you have any blueberry muffins or chocolate stuffed pastries? I like anything with sugar. I hope the gold coin I tossed into your cart is enough." Then I added, "Sorry about whacking you on the head with it. I didn't know you were in there." Another coin fell from my lips. I handed it to him.

"Oh my, you are adorable. Have a bag of my best muffins." He reached behind him and handed me a bag of muffins. I was so hungry I dove right into them without tasting anything. I even handed some muffins back to Charming and Edgar, who were still hiding in the bushes. They made disgusting chomping sounds while I smiled innocently at the muffin man.

"Are your friends okay?" the muffin man asked. "There is something familiar about that lumpy one. Why are they hiding in the bushes?"

"They're just shy," I said. "Well, thanks for the muffins." I bit into my muffin again and realized it was oat bran. So much for all the sugar I had hoped for. I dove into the bushes with Charming and Edgar. Together, we ran for the stables, chewing on healthy muffins as we went. "I asked for sugar," I complained.

"Bye!" the muffin man yelled after us.

"Maybe my sword is in the stable," Charming said. We opened the stable doors and crept inside. Edgar lit a torch, creating a warm circle of light around us.

I pointed to a stack of dirty gear. The smell alone was all I needed to convince me it belonged to the knights. Charming pulled a sword from the pile. He sighed in disappointment and put it back. "That's not it." Edgar joined him and pulled out another sword. Charming shook his head.

"What about this one?" I asked, pulling a sword from a separate pile.

Charming's face lit up. "That's it!" He took the sword and gazed at it adoringly.

"Why don't you just kiss it?" I asked. Why he was so excited about a stupid sword was beyond me.

He laughed and kissed the sword. A warm breeze blew through the stable, stirring up the scent of manure and sweaty animals. I covered my mouth. Sparkly lights appeared around Charming and swirled around him. His sword sent reflections of the sparkles all around us.

"What's going on?" I asked

Edgar shrugged. "No idea, but he's sparkling as much as Amy first thing in the morning. I hope it doesn't last too long. Someone is going to notice."

Charming rose from the ground, still surrounded by all the sparkles. His whiskers melted into his nose, and his fur vanished. Then his nose telescoped back into his face, and he was human again. His sword had been his true love all along. "Typical," I said. Boys and their swords. I would never understand it.

"Eric?" We all turned to find that the muffin man had followed us. So much for being stealthy. The muffin man saw Charming and gasped. "Eric, what happened to you? I could have sworn you were just a giant rat." He looked around wildly, his mouth wide open.

"Silence," Edgar said.

The muffin man opened his mouth, but no sound came out.

"You just silenced my best friend," Charming said.

"Your best friend grew up without you," Edgar said. "He's an adult now and not to be trusted."

"But you can't silence the muffin man," I said. "It's just wrong."

Edgar closed the stable doors. "Fine. Un-silence."

The muffin man cleared his throat. "Please don't call me the muffin man. I'm just Ferran." He turned to Charming. "What happened to you? You're just like I remember."

Charming glanced over at me. "I'm not really sure. I thought Raven cast a spell on me, but she's all princess. No magic."

How rude. "It was that magic combustion thing," I said, not bothering to hide my annoyance. I was not all princess. Sure, I choked out a coin now and then, but that hardly qualified me as *all princess*.

Ferran and Charming laughed.

"Magic combustion is a myth created by villains to keep heroes from helping each other," Ferran said. "Who told you that?"

I pointed to Edgar.

Edgar shrugged. "My dad told me."

"Who's your dad?" Ferran asked.

"Harold Perilous." Edgar shifted his feet. I didn't need our twin-thing to know what he was thinking. What else had our dad lied to us about?

"Harold Perilous?" Ferran repeated.

"Darkly," Charming explained. "He also cursed me to remain in the real world until I found my true love."

"Which is not me," I pointed out. I refused to feel insulted that he preferred a sword over me. We were enemies. It was natural. Plus he had the sword before he met me. "Speaking of which, you're human, and you have your sword. Shouldn't a magic portal labeled 'home' be opening up?"

Instead of a portal, the stable doors creaked open. The loathsome princess swept into the stable in a sparkling white wedding dress. "Ha! I found you!"

# Nineteen

The loathsome princess looked down her nose at Charming. "So you are human after all, and much better looking than Rodney." She tapped her bouquet against the side of her head and bit her lip. "Too bad you're so young." She turned to Ferran. "Do I know you?"

Ferran shook his head and stepped behind a pile of smelly gear.

She grabbed a lantern and held it up. "Are you married?"

Ferran's eyes widened. "I, uh." He looked around, panic all over his face. "I'm very poor. And I'm a peasant. A poor peasant."

She studied him for a moment through narrowed eyes. Then she shook her head. "You're cute, but I couldn't possibly marry a commoner. I can't marry Rodney either. He smells funny. I guess I'll just have to turn into an old maid tomorrow."

I couldn't imagine spending the rest of my life smelling Rodney either. "Why do you turn into an old maid tomorrow?"

The loathsome princess rolled her eyes and turned on me. "It's my twenty-first birthday, duh."

"How dare you talk to me like that!" I said. I motioned to Edgar to fry her revolting dress, but he was too busy admiring Charming's sword. Have I mentioned that we really needed to work on the whole twin-reading-each-other's-minds thing?

The loathsome princess smirked. "What are you going to do? Call the guards? You turn me in, you turn yourselves in." She sat on a saddle and smoothed out her silky white skirt. "So where are we going?"

"*We* aren't going anywhere," I said. "You can stay here and rot with Rodney. I am going back to the real world with my brother, and I guess Charming will go home with the muffin man."

"Ferran," the muffin man corrected.

The loathsome princess narrowed her eyes. "I knew I'd seen you before. You live on Drury Lane."

Ferran shook his head. "My brother is the muffin man now. I am headed off on an important mission."

"Yes!" Charming said, pumping his fist in the air. "Are you going to be my squire after all? I bet we could find a dragon or an evil sorceress to fight. We just need to—" He looked up at Ferran and his shoulders sagged. It was like watching a balloon deflate. "I used to be taller than you."

"You also used to be older." Ferran shook his head. Seeing Charming after all this time must have been pretty weird for him too. "I left Drury Lane to find a place to open a health food store. I have to follow my dreams."

I wrinkled my nose. That explained his oat muffins. Ew.

"You would like the real world," Charming said. "Healthy food is gaining popularity."

Not from me it wasn't.

"This is all very nice," the loathsome princess said, "but we should get going. They'll discover I'm missing pretty soon."

"They don't know you jilted Rodney?" I asked.

She shook her head.

The music outside suddenly stopped. A voice roared over the crowd. I didn't need to understand what they were saying. The meaning was clear: they'd discovered that the loathsome princess was missing. I resisted the urge to run outside and turn her in. It was almost worth being locked up in the dungeon again. Almost.

"Everyone in here," Edgar said, opening the door to a nearby empty stall. "We can hide under the straw."

"I'll go get my cart," Ferran said. "I'll park around back and sing the muffin man song when the coast is clear." He sighed. "I really need to learn a new song."

I dove under the straw. The stable was cleaner than the dungeon, but it was itchy. I missed my home. I was never sure what side of the house my room was going to be on, and my bedroom door occasionally opened to a cliff, but my bed was always warm and soft.

Heavy footsteps thundered through the stable. I curled into a ball, wishing I could do something. Fighting wasn't an option. They were all bigger than us and better equipped. Charming had a sword, but he couldn't hold off an entire army in their own castle.

The footsteps disappeared and silence surrounded us. A cart stopped outside, and Ferran's voice filtered in through the cracks in the stable wall.

"This way," the loathsome princess whispered.

We tiptoed through the stable, past nervous horses,

and out through a concealed door in the back. My cute new shoes didn't even fall off when I climbed into Ferran's muffin cart. I breathed in the sweet smell. Too bad there wasn't anything sweet left. It was all oat bran and wheat germ. Ew.

"There isn't enough room for me back here," Charming said.

"Sit up front with me." Ferran reached down and pulled Charming next to him. "No one saw you in human form." He threw a blanket over us. "Keep still back there."

Edgar gathered muffins and chomped them in the dark. "Sunflower seeds," he said. He chewed for a while. "I kinda like it."

"Ew," I said.

"Quiet, you two," the loathsome princess hissed. "If we get caught, I'll be forced to marry Rodney, and you will live out the rest of your lives in my dungeon."

We stopped talking.

The cart jerked forward. Edgar fell over and smashed his disgusting healthy muffin into my face. I brushed the wholesome mess off without a word.

"Ho, Muffin Man!"

Someone was stopping us. I grabbed Edgar's hand. It was sticky, but I didn't let go. Dungeons aren't my thing. The loathsome princess grabbed my other hand. It occurred to me that she probably had a real name, but it was a bad time to ask.

"I don't go by Muffin Man. Name's Ferran," Ferran said.

"We are searching for Princess Pansy."

I winced. What a terrible name. "Loathsome princess" was actually better. The rough wood from the bottom of the cart dug into my leg, and the blanket over us made it difficult to breathe, but I was smiling anyway. Her name was Pansy.

"Cold feet?" Ferran asked.

"Did you see the groom?" the guard asked. "I'm surprised she didn't bolt sooner."

"Where are you headed?" another gruff voice asked.

"I'm just trying to beat the crowd," Ferran said. "I'm all sold out of my sweet stuff, but I have some whole wheat barley muffins left. They're garnished with flax seeds." I silently gagged. Judging by the way Pansy was squeezing the life out of my hand, she was gagging too. "My apprentice here and I are going to set up a booth at the old witch's convention. You know how they get tired of gingerbread and sweets."

"You're clear to go, Muffin Man." The guard coughed. "We all know who you are anyway."

The cart lurched forward. We sat in silence as the noise from the castle grew distant and faded.

"Pansy," I snorted, unable to hold it in any longer. "Your name is Pansy."

"At least I'm not named after a filthy scavenger bird."

"Ravens are not filthy."

"They eat dead things."

"Pansy," I whispered, unable to come up with anything more clever. It had been a long day.

"I'm named after a poet," Edgar said. "He wrote about death and stuff." I really adore Edgar—as far as twin brothers go, he's not the worst—but there are times when I wish he'd keep his thoughts to himself.

The cart hit a rock and stopped.

"I can't breathe." Pansy pushed the blanket off our heads. We sat up to find ourselves surrounded by guards.

"Brilliant move," Charming said.

"It wasn't me." I pointed to Pansy. "She did it."

The cloaked woman I'd seen earlier with the king and queen stepped forward. Then, to my complete shock, Amy popped out from behind her. She put a finger to her lips and waved her pilfered wand. "Amy, what are you doing?" the cloaked woman asked. "Is that my new wand?" Her voice sounded familiar, but before I could figure out why, the guards and the old woman vanished and were replaced with happy trees.

The horse panicked and bolted. I held on to Edgar and closed my eyes. Magic wasn't as great as I'd always thought. In fact, I could do without another magic spell for the rest of my life.

"Calm down, Betsy," Ferran yelled.

Betsy continued to run, nearly plowing over a gentleman on a great white horse. The gentleman turned his horse and ran next to us, calming Betsy. "Whoa!"

Ferran got the horse under control, and we finally stopped. I jumped out of the cart, followed by Edgar and Pansy. Charming, who hadn't been subjected to riding under a blanket with Pansy, rubbed a speck of dust off his sword before jumping out of the cart and joining us.

"Hello," the gentleman said, looking at Pansy. "It looks like your horse got spooked."

"It's my horse," Ferran pointed out.

Pansy fluttered her eyelashes, which was even more disgusting than Ferran's oat muffins. "Thank you for stopping her. We are weary travelers looking for a safe place to stay tonight."

"You must stay with me," the gentleman said.

I grabbed an oat muffin and gnawed on it to offset the sickeningly sweet love-at-first-sight feelings in the air. *This* was not the kind of sugar I was craving.

"Oh, we couldn't impose." More eyelash fluttering.

"Gross," Charming whispered in my ear. I nodded.

"I hope your place is close," Pansy said. "I don't think I could ever get back in that cart." She rubbed her backside.

"It's close," the gentleman said. He nodded in Ferran's direction. "I've met the muffin man, but I've never had the pleasure of making your acquaintance before."

"Ferran," Ferran said. "I have a name, and I don't live on Drury Lane."

The gentleman nodded again and turned his eyes back to Pansy. "Everyone knows the muffin man."

"Pansy," I said. "Her name is Pansy. She's Princess Pansy." Then I added in one more "Pansy" for fun.

"I am Gregory, Pansy." He took her hand and kissed it. Edgar and Charming made gagging noises. "Pansies are my favorite flower."

I rolled my eyes. Oh please. No one likes pansies that much. People just plant them because they like cool weather and are easy to grow.

"The muffin man and his little friends were helping me escape from a most terrible fate." Pansy clasped her hands together and fluttered her eyelashes in a helpless manner. I loved how she skipped the part where she had me locked in a dungeon and manipulated her way into marrying Rodney, only to change her mind once she caught a whiff of him.

"I too have averted a terrible marriage today." The gentleman gave her an understanding yet sad smile. I silently thanked my parents for letting me grow up in the real world.

A white kitten streaked down the road and ran up the gentleman's leg. "Hello, Angel," he said, peeling the kitten off his leg.

Charming and I exchanged shocked looks with Edgar. We'd met that kitten before.

"We can't let them get together," I whispered. "Poor little Ella would get Pansy for a stepmother."

"Don't you dare break up another wedding," Charming whispered back.

I raised an eyebrow.

"I know they aren't engaged yet, but this is the Enchanted Forest. True love hits like the stomach flu around here." Charming glanced over at Pansy and Gregory. "Ella will get an evil stepmother, but her father is safe. Pansy actually likes him. It's better this way."

"But . . ."

Charming shook his head. "Not a word. She doesn't have daughters. Ella will grow up in a castle and still have a chance to meet her prince."

I made a face.

"Not that you care about true love."

"You're one to talk. You're in love with a sword."

He grinned and ran his finger over the hilt. "I'm also thirteen. Pansy and Gregory are adults."

"Fine." I cleared my throat. "I'd rather have Pansy stay here anyway. She doesn't exactly belong in the real world."

"Angel!" Ella ran down the path and stopped when she saw us. She took the kitten from her father and buried her face in its fur. "Naughty kitten. Stay with me."

I knelt next to Ella and whispered, "Pansy is probably going to be your new stepmother. She really likes dragons."

Ella nodded. "Oh good. I found a new dragon friend in the forest today. He wears orange tutus so he must be nice."

"I know that dragon," I whispered back. "I bet your new stepmother would love to meet him."

We waved good-bye to Pansy, climbed in the cart, and headed back to the gingerbread house. Betsy clomped along at a steady pace until we reached the clearing, then she stopped and snorted. Lady Laurel and Amy were waiting for us there.

"Wasn't Amy just with the evil witch?" I whispered to Charming.

"Look at the robe Lady Laurel has thrown over her arm," Charming whispered back. "I think Amy is still with the evil witch."

"I also have very good hearing," Lady Laurel said. She waved her arm, and her fluffy blue hair turned white as her pretty wrinkled face turned haggard.

"Wow," Charming said. "She's hideous."

"Are you going to let him talk about your grandmother that way?" the witch asked me.

Edgar and I exchanged looks of horror. "You're our Grandma Perilous?" I asked.

"Who else would be so anxious to welcome the Perilous twins into the Enchanted Forest?" the old lady screeched.

# Twenty

Grandma Perilous cackled at our surprise. "I kidnapped your mother for a reason. Her jewels were going to make me rich. I would have everything I ever wanted. So when her time with me was due to end, I arranged for Mr. Right to get lost." She grinned, showing off yellow teeth. "He turned left instead of right. Since he had failed, a magical calling went out to a knight in shining armor. He put up a better fight, but he ultimately scuttled off into the shadows as well. The closest prince charming was an infant, so I knew I would have plenty of time before another hero came along. And by then, I would be the richest witch in the west, so to speak."

"I was not an infant," Charming said. "I was eight when the magical calling came—almost nine."

Grandma Perilous sniffed. "Close enough. Then my good-for-nothing son had to feel sorry for Charming and the princess. He found a way into the real world and brought them both with him. I swore he would regret the day he helped Butterfly escape. Seven years of jewels was not nearly enough. Butterfly was pretty stingy with her tears."

"Why did you bring us here?" Edgar asked.

"You obviously take after your father, intelligence-wise, Edgar. Such a disappointment. I followed your parents to the real world after they escaped the Enchanted Forest so I could find a way to recapture the princess. It was too late to capture her, since married princesses are off limits, but then they had a daughter, and she was fair game."

"It took you fourteen years to capture a princess?" Charming asked. "That's not very impressive."

"Raven listened to her mother and never wandered into the woods as a small child, so I couldn't get my hands on her. Who ever heard of such an obedient child? Then she decided to be evil, and evil girls are never locked in towers. I knew Raven's princess genes would eventually take over and make her nice. It's taken me fourteen years, but I finally have my princess, and every one of her beautiful, sparkly tears will add to my fortune."

"I'm no one's princess," I said. "Especially not yours."

"Oh, but you are." She waved her arm, and my jeans were replaced with a fluffy pink princess dress. A heavy tiara settled on my head.

"We shouldn't have trusted you." I pulled on the tiara, but it wouldn't budge. "I should have known you were evil. The shoes you gave me always fell off my feet."

"The shoes were infused with evil so even if you decided to become good, you would spew slugs and frogs instead of jewels. That way your parents would never suspect that you were my target. Of course, they never guessed that sweet Lady Laurel was actually the evil witch. Your mother used to cry sad little diamond tears every time the evil witch caught her after her dear fairy godmother helped her escape. Then I collected the beauties and left her to weep some more."

No wonder my mom was always so happy. Nothing compared to the horrors she'd experienced in the clutches of her future mother-in-law.

Suddenly, plain gold necklaces appeared on my neck, and rings with empty claws covered my fingers. I fell to my knees, unable to stay upright under so much weight in gold.

"Do you like my golden pretties? They are charmed to catch every last diamond tear that falls from your sad little cheeks. Once a strand or ring is full, it will vanish and come to me. Don't worry, though. I'll replace them."

"Leave her alone!" Edgar yelled. He ran to my side and pulled on a necklace. It took some pressure off my chest, but he couldn't remove it. "You're hurting her. All you do is hurt our family. You kidnapped my mother and lied to my dad about magic. Why would you do that? You could have made a fortune selling spells with Dad's help."

"Selling spells?" Grandma Perilous scoffed. "People buy one or two spells, and then they form a mob and torch your home when someone breaks out into a rash or turns into a newt. Jewels don't shake pitchforks at you. I originally made up the magical reaction story to keep your father away from the princess. His pathetic, soft heart made him worry about the poor little baby Prince Charming too. But instead of staying away, he helped Butterfly escape the forest."

Charming bristled but didn't say anything.

"That same lie made it possible for me to take Charming out of the picture without risking an immediate undo spell. Then I was betrayed by my own servant." She paused to glare at Amy.

"I didn't betray you," Amy said defensively. "I followed most of your orders."

"Your understanding of magic might have made me proud if you weren't fighting me at every turn. Stealing a real wand was genius. I almost regret the need to punish you."

Amy shrank back from the witch. I knew she'd been on my side the whole time. I wanted to say something, but the heavy gold necklaces were cutting off my oxygen supply. Grandma Perilous looked at me and bared her yellow teeth in what may have been a smile. "My tower is all ready for you."

Charming let out a roar, lifted his sword over his head, and rushed the old witch. She sent his sword flying into the trees with a simple swish of her wand. Charming ran after it.

Amy stood over me, tears gushing down her cheeks. "Amy," I gasped. It sounded a lot more pathetic than I wanted it to.

"I'm sorry," Amy said. She fiddled with the flower jewel on her shirt. "I'm so sorry. She made me do it."

"As for you," the witch said, turning to Amy. "You used your small knowledge of magic to temporarily undo my rat spell, and you've been cancelling out the evil spell I put on Raven's shoes. You betrayed me."

Amy shook her head. "I had to mess with your rat spell. The owner of the climbing gym was waiting to make sure all three of us left so he could lock up."

Grandma Perilous took a menacing step toward Amy. "You thought I wouldn't notice when you stole my wand and helped them to the top of that tower or when you sent them here the moment they were in my clutches. It's time for you to see what happens to useless peasant girls who defy me."

Amy's flower jewel started to glow. Her eyes bulged, and her skin turned a brilliant emerald green. Spikes grew out of her head and tore through the back of her shirt. Soon she was a giant lizard.

"What did you do to Sparklepants?" Edgar asked.

The giant lizard flicked her tongue and wrapped it around Edgar. Spots appeared before my eyes. The pressure on my chest from all the necklaces was too much. I gasped for air.

"You won't be any good to me dead," Grandma Perilous said to me. The weight lifted enough for me to breathe, but not enough for me to move. I lifted my head in time to see Amy's tail disappear into the trees. Edgar was gone. I hoped she wouldn't eat him.

Grandma Perilous looked around. "Come back here, you useless peasant!" she yelled. "Now I need someone to help me get you to the tower." She waved her wand, and a sparkly circle appeared. The circle stretched, and the giant lumberjack statue stepped through it. Ferran ran out of nowhere and jumped into the circle before it closed with a snap. I'd forgotten all about him. He was definitely a better muffin man than a hero, despite his wheat germ muffins. Even the muffin man had abandoned me. I was alone with Grandma Perilous and a giant lumberjack.

"The lumberjack will watch you while I go after your brother. I need to replace my servant, and I was hoping to keep it in the family."

The lumberjack stepped forward and lifted me into a giant hug, pinning my arms to my sides. I kicked, but I may as well have been kicking a log. It didn't even grunt.

Grandma Perilous snapped her fingers, and the gingerbread house sprouted giant chicken legs. She stood in the doorway while the house lumbered to its feet. Then it ran in the direction Amy and Edgar had gone, the house staying far above the trees. I hoped it would trip and send Grandma into a river.

Charming ran back into the clearing, holding his sword high above his head. "Blasted witch." He glanced up at me. "No offense."

"I'm not a witch!" I yelled.

"I know. I just insulted your grandmother."

"Oh." I struggled to free myself from the creepy lumberjack. It stared down at me with its one painted eye. The view under his splintery nostrils was unpleasant.

Charming watched me struggle for a moment. "Need some help?"

I wriggled an arm free, only to have the lumberjack snatch it back. "No, I'm fine."

"Your brother might need some help."

I swung my leg up to the lumberjack's arm and pushed. The lumberjack grabbed my leg and held me still.

Charming slashed the lumberjack's arm with his sword. The arm fell off, and I landed with a thump on the ground. I tried to sit up, but the jewels were too heavy. I couldn't even lift my head. "I told you I didn't need any help."

Charming sighed. "I wasn't helping you. I was helping myself. That was too painful to watch."

The lumberjack bent forward to snatch me with its remaining arm. I slowly rolled away as it grabbed at my slippery skirts. Charming stepped forward and hacked off the lumberjack's other arm.

Charming stood over me, his head cocked to the side, and grinned his stupid, handsome smile. "Maybe I could help you with those jewels. It wouldn't be a rescue, more like a recovery."

"Shows what you know," I scoffed. "A recovery is what they call a rescue when all hope is lost." My skirt was puffed up so high, it almost reached the lumberjack's knees. The lumberjack shuddered and two arms popped out of its side. Each arm held an ax. "What did you do, Charming?" Two more arms popped out of the other side, each with an ax. "Duck!"

Charming ducked and rolled as the lumberjack swung at him. Then it set its one-eyed gaze on me. The place where the second eye had flaked away glowed red.

"I think we've reached recovery status," I said.

"Move the necklaces to the side of your head so I don't hit you." Charming hacked a leg off the lumberjack. It slowly creaked and then fell over.

"I don't know if you should have done that." I pushed the necklaces over my shoulder and held my breath.

Charming swung his sword, breaking the necklaces with a flash of blinding light. I took a deep breath and hurried to my feet. The rings wouldn't come off, but at least I could maneuver. The lumberjack shuddered, and two new legs popped out. It now had four arms and three legs. The ground shook as it got to its feet.

"Should we run for it?" Charming asked.

The lumberjack turned toward me, bathing me in the red light of its missing eye. "Yes! Run!" We ran for the trees, my skirts swishing around my ankles. The lumberjack threw an ax over our heads and hit a tree branch over the path. The branch snapped and fell in front of us, blocking the path. The trees were too thick to go around. We were stuck.

"Now what?" Charming ducked as the lumberjack threw another ax at us.

"I wish Edgar was here with his fireballs." The lumberjack suddenly rushed forward with a burst of speed, but the extra leg made it go faster on one side, so it went around in a circle instead of getting closer. It was actually pretty pathetic. "I think we could find a way around the branch. That thing is never going to catch up to us."

The lumberjack's red light cast eerie shadows over its unnaturally large smile. Two new axes appeared in its hands. One ax flashed in the light of the disappearing sun as the lumberjack cut off its own leg with a sickening thud. Charming and I exchanged worried looks. The side with two legs had been pretty fast. Our chance for escape would vanish as soon as it generated another pair of legs.

"I wish Edgar was here too, or Ferran. Ferran always carried a fire starter kit with him."

"Ferran ran into the real world when the witch brought the lumberjack here."

Charming looked over at the muffin cart, which was only a few feet away. Realization dawned on his face. We both rushed for the cart.

"We need fuel." I yanked the blanket off the back, uncovering all the healthy muffins. "Do muffins burn?"

Charming pulled a small metal box out from under the driver's seat. Betsy stomped on the ground, her ears laid back. The lumberjack swung its head around, shining red light on us.

"Go on, Betsy." Charming unhooked the bridle and gave her a firm pat on the rump. She ran for the woods. The sky was turning pink in the west. It would be dark soon. We had to hurry if we were ever going to find Edgar and Amy.

The cart tilted as Charming climbed into the back with me. "Hold out a muffin. I'll light it, and then you throw it at the lumberjack."

I shook my head. "No way. I'm not fireproof. You have the wrong twin for that."

The lumberjack shuddered.

"We're running out of time. Those extra legs are going to pop out any second now, and we'll be toast." Charming grabbed a muffin. "We have to get the burning muffin to the lumberjack somehow." I knocked the muffin from his hand. "Don't you dare get all heroic on me and sacrifice your hands for the cause. You aren't enchanted any more. You can get hurt now."

Two more legs popped out of the lumberjack.

"We have to do something now." Charming grabbed my arm and pulled me behind the cart, out of the lumberjack's view. Red light swept across the meadow.

"All my life I've planned escapes from towers," I said. Annoying diamond tears rolled down my face and were sucked into the rings on my fingers. The rings vanished, but they weren't replaced. The witch must have been busy. "No one told me there would be dungeons and lumberjacks and . . . and . . . tooth fairies." I sniffed. "Wait." I unwrapped my carabiner from around my wrist. "I still have this." I dug the carabiner into a muffin. The lumberjack charged, knocking the cart over. We landed on the ground with the cart over our heads.

The ground rumbled. "Are you all right?" I whispered to Charming.

"I'm fine," Charming whispered back. "Now what do we do?"

I didn't have time to answer. The cart tilted and axes crashed into the wood above us. We gathered as many muffins as we could hold and ran out from under the cart. The lumberjack roared and slammed the cart back down. Its one good eye settled on us.

"Light the muffin," I said.

Charming hit two stones together, creating a cute little spark that was as useful as a cute little tooth fairy. The muffin wasn't even singed. The lumberjack held its axes high and rushed for us. We ran behind what was left of the cart. With its intense speed and extra legs, the lumberjack couldn't stop. It rammed into a tree on the far side of the meadow. The tree crashed to the ground.

"There goes another path," I said.

"We need real kindling," Charming said. "The muffin won't burn."

I pointed to the cart we were cowering behind. "How about this?"

"Ferran is not going to like this."

"Ferran ran away," I pointed out.

Charming hit the stones together, and another tiny spark appeared.

"I thought you knew how to use that thing."

"Fire was never my strong point," Charming said.

The lumberjack was back on its feet. It lowered its head and rushed the cart. I grabbed Charming's arm, and we ran. The lumberjack plowed through the cart like a semi-truck plowing through a Volvo. So much for our cover.

I grabbed some dry pine needles and crammed them in the muffin like tiny birthday candles. "Keep trying."

Charming held the stones over the muffin and hit them together with all his might. This time a bigger spark appeared, and a pine needle caught fire. The needle quickly burst into flames and spread to the other needles. I held my breath, hoping the muffin would burn too. The pine needles burned down, but the muffin didn't catch fire.

Charming grabbed a stick and held it to the end of the needles before they all burned out. Flames curled around the stick. I extinguished the needles and wrapped the carabiner and rope around my wrist.

I grabbed a handful of twigs and lit them on fire with Charming's stick. Then he tossed one at the lumberjack. The stick hit the massive statue and fell to the ground, extinguishing the fire. The lumberjack turned toward us.

"I have an idea," Charming whispered.

"Why are you whispering? It can see our burning sticks."

"Just trust me." Charming grabbed my hand and dragged me around the edge of the meadow. The lumberjack slammed into the tree we had just been standing under. "Get ready to run."

"Out in the open? Didn't you notice how fast that thing is?" I wanted to pull my hand back, but I didn't. Charming wasn't trying to save me. We were working together. It was a group effort. My stupid fluffy skirt made me less useful than Charming, but I had managed to find some kindling.

We ran to the biggest chunk of wreckage from the cart. Charming set his flaming sticks on the cart and then placed the rest of my burning sticks on top. We rushed across the meadow to the safety of the trees. The dry wooden cart quickly caught fire.

"Brilliant move," I whispered. "We'll never be subject to healthy muffins again. But what about the lumberjack?"

Charming pulled me to the side. The burning cart was directly between us and the lumberjack. He raised his hands over his head and yelled, "Hey, you pile of over-grown toothpicks!"

"We're trying to avoid getting killed by the lumberjack." I grabbed his arm and tried to make him stop waving.

A narrow beam of red light settled on our heads. "Get ready to jump," Charming said.

The lumberjack rushed at us in a straight line, plowing into the burning cart. Flames appeared on the lumberjack's legs. We jumped out of the way before it crashed into a tree. Charming grabbed my hand, and we ran across the meadow again. The lumberjack followed, but its legs turned to ash as it ran. It fell on a burning crate crammed with healthy muffins.

Charming pointed his sword at the forest. "Time to go save your brother."

I climbed over the log blocking the path, pausing only to rip my fluffy skirt free from the rough wood. Then I ran into the forest with Prince Charming.

# Twenty-One

Charming ran his hand over the flat of his sword as we followed the path into the woods. "You're going to cut yourself with that," I said.

"I think I nicked the blade cutting those necklaces off you."

I grabbed his arm and squinted at the sword in the dim light. "I don't see anything."

"You wouldn't." He held his sword close to his chest.

I felt a little guilty for dismissing his sword so quickly. After all, it was his true love. And he'd used it to free me from those necklaces. A branch snagged my skirt. Charming kept walking. "Wait!" I yanked the skirt, smiling when it ripped and ran to catch up. "Let me see again."

He held the sword up in the fading sunlight and pointed. There was a tiny spot that might have been a ding on the blade. "I see it." I pointed at the ding. "I guess magic gold is hard on steel. Thanks for saving me." An emerald fell from my lips and was sucked up by another ring. The ring vanished. My skirt snagged again. This time Charming waited for me to yank it back.

The path narrowed, and my skirt caught on every branch. The trees closed in around us. I stepped forward, but the skirt was too wide to fit through. It wedged between trees, so I couldn't back out either. I was stuck.

"Do you have anything on under the skirt?" Charming asked.

I felt my cheeks heat up. "What kind of question is that?"

Charming cleared his throat. "I just thought that maybe I could cut the skirt off you, and then we could go on."

Since I wasn't the one who put the outfit on, I had no idea what I had on under the skirt. There was something there, and it was pretty itchy. "Do it. Cut this stupid skirt off of me. But close your eyes, just in case."

"I can't use my sword with my eyes closed. How about I make some holes and you rip while my back is turned?" Charming grabbed a handful of material and sawed back and forth. Nothing happened. I shouldn't have been surprised. He held it away from my legs and tried stabbing. No luck. His sword would only slide along the pink material. Every rip I'd put in it had vanished. I should have made use of them while they were there.

"It catches on every branch, but a sword can't penetrate it?" Charming scratched his head. "Magic is so confusing."

I yanked at the skirt. The last time I got caught by a tree, it was because of my hair. I could only be grateful that my dad and his cockroach weren't nearby. A knot formed in my stomach as I realized there was no way out. I was helpless.

"I'll go ahead, save Edgar, and come back for you with him," Charming said. "He'll know what to do."

I nodded as a diamond tear slid down my cheek and disappeared into a ring. "I wish I had a real fairy godmother who actually wanted to help me. I could use a wardrobe change."

Charming laughed. "I'll be fast."

He ran off into the forest, leaving me alone with my skirt. Branches crackled off in the distance.

"Hello?" I called.

Silence.

"If you're a princess-eating beast, you should know I'm smaller than the average princess. I'm hardly worth the effort."

More branches crackled, and I had the feeling someone was watching me. My legs shook. I yanked my skirt, frantically trying to free myself. I needed help. My lips formed the words, but no sound came out. I couldn't bring myself to ask for help out loud.

White sparks danced around me and joined together in a massive ball of light. When the light faded, Ms. Darkwing stood before me. Now I was alone with a nameless beast in the woods and an evil vice principal.

"There you are." She smiled and held her wand up. It was the same heart-shaped pencil that Amy had carried around. "Look! I found my wand."

I sighed. "Fine. Lock me up in a tower or dungeon. Anything is better than this."

She shook her head. "Why would I do that? I'm your fairy godmother."

I raised an eyebrow (because that was all I could move at the moment.) "You're my fairy godmother?"

"Of course. We like to keep quiet about who we really are, especially after Cinderella. Suddenly, every girl thinks she needs a new dress for every dance. It gets tiresome. We only reveal our identities in extreme circumstances, and I have no worries about you demanding an extended wardrobe."

"Then why did you have the lumberjack drag me off to the Enchanted Forest? That's not something a fairy godmother would do."

"That wasn't me. The Perilous witch enchanted the lumberjack. She also broke my old wand, and the new one took a lot longer to come than it should have. I suspected that Amy had it. That's why I kept asking you where she was."

"But Amy returned your wand this morning. Why did it take you so long to find us? Edgar . . ." I swallowed hard. Amy wouldn't really eat him, even if he called her Sparklepants—I hoped.

"She gave it to the muffin man, and he just barely brought it to me."

"Well, that was a roundabout way to get your wand back to you."

Ms. Darkwing smiled. "She told him she wanted to be sure that I got it and couldn't safely deliver it herself. The muffin man was a logical choice. Everyone knows the muffin man. He—"

"—lived on Drury Lane." I finished for her. "That must be a busy road. He could have told us he had your wand."

"He didn't know you were connected until after Amy sent you back to the meadow. All he could do was make use of his first opportunity to get out of the Enchanted Forest."

"Is that why he didn't come back with you?"

"I sent him to find your parents and let them know we're working on getting you home. He also had to find someone named Betsy." Ms. Darkwing paced along the path, tapping her chin with her wand. "Now then, I've been watching you at school, and to be honest, I can't decide if you're evil or good. Only nice girls get fairy godmothers."

"What?" I sounded shocked, but I wasn't sure either. My biggest fear was once getting locked in a tower, but never seeing my family again seemed worse. Being evil used to be the most important thing to me, but suddenly, even Charming and Amy meant more. I'd also learned that supposedly "good" damsels in distress could really be rotten, like Pansy.

"I can help only the good girls. I'm sure you understand."

I did not like where this was going. Someone had finally accepted that I might be evil, instead of just cute, but now I didn't want to be evil. I wanted to be good—or at least *mostly* good.

"In the interest of time, I've devised a quick little test. Ready?"

I shook my head. "I can't even move, Ms. Darkwing. The trees have closed in on me."

Charming appeared on the path behind her. He cocked his head to the side but didn't say anything.

"No worries. I don't need you to do anything. I just need to know the name of this boy." A tiny figurine of the boy from the bus appeared in her hand.

"Oh, well. Umm. I know that boy, but I don't have time for this. I need to rescue my brother."

"Who is evil," Ms. Darkwing said.

"And Amy."

"Also probably evil."

"She really likes puppies and volunteers at the shelter on a regular basis."

Ms. Darkwing took a deep breath. "We're testing your evilness, not theirs."

"But they need my help."

"Name the boy." Ms. Darkwing held up the figurine. "Good people care for those around them. He's been in almost every class with you since kindergarten. It's not that hard of a test."

Easy for her to say. Ever since I found out I was destined to be rescued by a boy, I ignored every one I met. This boy's name started with a hard consonant, like a C or a Q. Charming waved at me from behind Ms. Darkwing. I waggled my eyebrows, which was almost like waving back.

Charming lifted one of his legs to the side and held an arm up. I was about to ask him if he was injured when I realized he was making a letter with his body.

"K!" I yelled. "His name starts with a K."

Ms. Darkwing nodded. "Well, yes. Just tell me his name. You don't have to spell it."

"I want to prove that I know his name so well I can spell it."

Charming stood sideways and held both arms and one leg out in front of him. "Three?" His eyes widened, and he faced the other direction. "Er, I mean three rhymes with E. The next letter is E." I tried to put the two letters together in my head, but no name formed behind it. Why did this boy have such a difficult name?

Charming held his arms at an angle over his head. "Y?" He shook his head and dropped to the ground. His arms and legs shot up as he balanced on his bottom.

"My question exactly," Ms. Darkwing said. "Why are you taking so long?"

"V," I said quickly. "Kev . . ." Ms. Darkwing leaned forward, and Charming jumped up with his hands in the air to form an I. "Kevin!" I said. "His name is Kevin, of course."

"Yes," Ms. Darkwing said. "That's right." She waved her wand, and the pink fluffy dress of doom was replaced with a soft leather tunic and leggings. I stepped away from the trees.

"Practical clothes are nice." These ones weren't my style, but they were definitely an improvement. "But what we really need is for all of us to be zapped home."

Ms. Darkwing smiled. "You can't go home until your journey is through." She turned around. "Hello, Eric."

Charming smiled and leaned against a tree.

"It is nice to see you two working together. You both passed my test." She patted Charming's shoulder. "Oh, Raven, I almost forgot. I talked to your mother this morning after that unfortunate incident with the lumberjack. She asked me to remind you that jewels are a princess's number one tool." Then she vanished.

She had to be joking. I'd barely escaped all those necklaces with my life. Jewels got in the way.

"If I'd known I was allowed to help you, I would have just told you his name." Charming brushed dead leaves from off his backside as we followed the path. "Although I don't know how you keep forgetting it. You've known him forever."

I shrugged. "He isn't horrible, as far as boys go. I'm sure he'll even be tolerable in a couple of years."

Charming was quiet for a while. A cool evening breeze rustled the leaves around us. "What about me?"

"What about you?" I glanced at him from the corner of my eye. His hair was backlit by the sunset. I quickly looked away. Walking with a boy at sunset could be dangerous.

"Are we enemies?"

"No." I thought for a moment. "You're already tolerable.

Your Charming genes must be kicking in." I bumped his arm with my elbow.

He bumped my shoulder with his arm. "Let's go rescue Edgar and Amy."

The path widened, and a massive cliff hid what was left of the setting sun. I couldn't help but grin as I took the carabiner off my wrist. "Finally we get to climb." Years of preparation were about to pay off.

# Twenty-Two

I slid the carabiner off my wrist and kissed it.

Charming laughed.

"What?" I wiped a little smudge of dirt off the clip.

"You think I'm weird for loving my sword. You love a magic carabiner."

"And its accompanying rope." I tossed the carabiner in the air, and it wrapped the magic rope several times around a stone high on the cliff before securing itself. "You have to admit that it's useful." I grabbed the rope and gave it a little tug. It was secure.

Charming put his hand on my shoulder before I could climb. "Wait. I should go first."

"Why?"

"That stone isn't all the way at the top. We'll have to do a little free climbing. It's hard to tell the distance from down here."

I wanted to argue, but he was right. There wasn't any way to determine the distance from the stone to the top. Charming, being the tallest, had the best chance of getting over the cliff. He wasn't trying to rescue me. He was looking out for me and our mission, which was actually kind of sweet in a nonromantic kind of way.

"Go ahead," I said.

He let out a big breath. He must have been worried I'd fight him. I couldn't imagine why. I'm a pretty reasonable person.

The cliff was full of holes and protruding rocks. Charming scurried up the first part without any problem. Then he reached smooth rock. He held the rope in both hands, but his feet kept slipping.

"Slide your foot to the left," I yelled.

Charming slid his foot to the left where a small rock jutted out.

I hoped his arms weren't getting tired. "Your right foot needs to reach a little higher."

He found the spot.

I called directions out to him until he reached the protruding stone where the rope was secured. It was no wonder Amy was so good at climbing, if this was the cliff she had to work with.

"There's a ledge up here," Charming said. He swung his leg up and over a narrow ledge. Tiny rocks rolled down the face of the cliff as he scurried over the side. The top of the cliff was chest high to him. I probably wouldn't have been able to reach it. He took the rope off the rock and secured it around his shoulder before finishing the climb. Then he lowered the rope to me.

"There isn't anything up here to secure it to. I'll have to pull you up."

I tied the rope around my waist for safety. My hands needed to be free so I could climb. "Just anchor it for me," I yelled to Charming. "You need your strength to fight my grandma."

"It sounds so noble when you put it that way," he yelled back.

I grinned and started climbing. The first part was as easy as it looked. The second part was not so easy. As the anchor, Charming had to stay away from the edge of the cliff, so he couldn't help me the way I had helped him. I slid my hand up the smooth face until I found a sturdy rock. Then I did the same thing with my foot. My new shoes gripped the cliff like no shoe had ever gripped before. I wondered if I could find the homeless elf that made these shoes and bring him home with me.

My hand hit the ledge, and I swung my leg up. There was barely enough room for me to get back to a standing position. "I'm on the ledge," I called. Charming's face appeared over the side. He held his hand out to me. I took it and let him pull me up. "Thanks, Charming. You're every bit as useful as a carabiner."

"Just don't kiss me." He smiled, showing off his dimpled cheek.

I snorted. No danger there. "I'd rather kiss a rat." This time we both laughed. Truth be told, if the world was about to end and the only thing that would save everyone was if I kissed him, I'd seriously consider it. I untied the rope and let it retract until all I had was a shiny carabiner.

We followed the tree line until we found a path. I had the strangest feeling that whatever had been with me in the woods before Ms. Darkwing appeared was still following me, but I couldn't see anyone behind us. The sun finished slipping behind the horizon, and a full moon appeared. It was brighter than the moon in the real world. I could see the trees and Charming without any problem. It was just the ground that was impossible to see. I tripped and crashed into Charming. "I miss sidewalks."

"Me too." He rubbed his back where I'd head-butted him.

"Sorry." A massive diamond the size of my fist fell from my lips. It clinked on one of the empty rings, but it was too big for the claw and fell to the forest floor. I retrieved it and stuffed it in a pocket. I could accept being sort of good, but I didn't want to admit that I'd said something nice enough to warrant a diamond that size. Being evil was part of who I was.

A branch snapped behind us. "Do you have the feeling someone is following us?" I whispered to Charming.

An owl hooted in a tree above our heads. Charming jumped and then laughed. "I'm sure it's just an animal. Are your woods this spooky at night?"

"I don't go in the woods due to the abundance of man-eating beasts." I turned around but couldn't see anyone behind us.

"I wonder if I could find a way to survive in your real world."

For some reason I liked that idea. Life with Charming was definitely interesting. "Maybe. You'd have to find an adult to take you in, though."

"Why? I've been on my own for almost a year now. I knew I might not see my parents again after I waved good-bye."

"You get to be a kid longer in the real world. Some people aren't really adults until they're in their twenties." I stepped around a root sticking out of the ground. "Kids are never sent out in the woods without supervision, and there are laws about kids being alone."

"Two days ago I was hoping the princess I had to rescue wasn't a snorer."

I laughed because my mom would be horrified if anyone knew she snored. "That was more like fourteen years ago."

"To you. It's only been a few days for me."

"Ms. Darkwing got you into the school in the first place, didn't she?"

"Yes."

"Maybe she could help you find a permanent home so you could stay."

He nodded but didn't say anything. It never occurred to me that princes had an equally rotten deal as the princesses. They could rescue a princess, just to be nice, and get stuck with someone like Pansy in Happily Ever After. Ew.

The trees thinned out, and the path opened into another meadow, only this one had a dark tower on the far end. A giant lizard perched on top of it. There was no sign of Edgar or Grandma Perilous, but they had to be close.

"Edgar!" I ran for the tower.

"Raven!" Charming grabbed my arm and yanked me backward as the lizard ran down the side of the tower.

"I have to find Edgar." I pulled my arm back, but I couldn't get Charming to release me. "He's here somewhere. Then we can find a way to save Amy." We could never wear matching shoes if she was a giant lizard.

Charming dragged me back to the trees. The lizard ran across the meadow, its tongue flickering in and out of its mouth.

"Amy wasn't safe to be around when she was human," Charming whispered. "Now she's deadly."

The flower jewel glinted in the moonlight. "Grandma Perilous has a weird thing for jewels. That flower must be part of her enchantment. We have to get it off her."

"How do you plan to do that?"

"I'll distract her while you sneak up from the side and knock the jewel off."

Charming snorted. "You've got to be kidding."

"I don't kid."

Amy flicked her tongue in our direction and came running at us. Her eyes glinted red in the moonlight.

Charming threw a stick at her. The stick hit the jewel but didn't knock it off. Amy ran into the meadow. I searched the ground for something else to throw, but there was nothing but dried leaves around me. Charming searched his pockets and found the rock he'd put there when we first arrived in the Enchanted Forest.

We circled the tree, keeping low. Amy was only a few feet away. It wouldn't take her long to find us.

Charming took aim and threw the rock at Amy. It soared through the air and smashed into the jewel. The jewel fell to the ground with a thud. The red gleam left Amy's eyes, but she remained a lizard.

"Why isn't she human?" I asked.

"I don't know. She's your friend."

"Maybe she needs a kiss."

"You've got to be kidding."

Edgar wouldn't do it either, even if I knew where he was. "Amy," I said in a nice calm voice. "Please don't eat me."

Amy looked over at me, but she wasn't Amy anymore. She was just a dumb lizard that was also very big and scary.

"Hey, Sparklepants!" Edgar leaned out the tower window. I would have laughed if it hadn't all been so scary. It was about time Edgar got the wrong end of the twin thing. "Sparklepants! Where are you?"

Something sparked in the eyes of the lizard. Amy was in there somewhere. She turned and ran across the field toward the tower. Edgar ducked back inside.

"At least we know Edgar is fine." I ran over to the ground where the jewel had fallen. It was a bright splash of red in the moonlight.

"Don't touch it!" Charming yelled. "You don't know what it'll do to you."

"But it's the key to turning Amy back into herself."

"Are you sure you want her to be human again?" Charming asked. "She can't do any magic as a lizard."

I chose to ignore his comment. "I think you'll have to break the jewel."

"How?"

"Use your sword."

"Are you kidding?"

"You keep asking me that. I already told you I don't kid."

"Breaking those necklaces put a nick in my sword. Breaking a cursed jewel could destroy it."

I didn't answer him because something lifted me off my feet. Amy had sneaked back and wrapped her tongue around my waist. It was as disgusting as it sounded. I'm not ashamed to admit that I screamed as she pulled me to her mouth. Without the jewel to control her, she could easily have me as a light snack. "Break the stupid jewel!" Charming lifted his sword. His lip might have trembled a bit, but it was too dark to be sure.

At that moment I realized what I was asking him to do. His friends were grown up. His family thought he was dead. He didn't even have a home. The sword was all he had, and he loved it. "No! Wait!" I struggled, hoping to find a way to escape, but it was too late.

Charming lifted his sword and stabbed the jewel with a loud clunk. A red glow from the jewel crept up the sword. The air crackled, and I suddenly fell to the ground. A red light flashed, leaving us blind in the darkness. Amy was gone, and Charming's sword was probably broken forever.

# Twenty-Three

Charming showed no emotion as the evil red light fled the broken jewel and crept up his sword. A thick mist surrounded us, making it difficult to breathe. My muscles ached from all the climbing and walking. "You have to fight the spell!" I yelled.

Charming shook his head. "How can I? I don't have any magic." His voice was thick with emotion.

I collapsed, landing on my side. Something hard dug into my leg. I reached into my pocket and pulled out the diamond. Moonlight sparkled in its perfect face, a symbol of my total lack of evilness. I got up and forced my way through a mist of magic to him. What I was about to do would mean that I'd have to let go of my bad girl image forever.

I collapsed next to Charming and touched the blade with the diamond. Blue light swirled out of the diamond and danced around the red light, turning the sword a glowing purple. When the light faded, the mist was gone. Charming held his sword up to the moonlight.

"It doesn't look broken, but why is there a hole in the hilt?"

I handed him the diamond. "Put this in the hole."

Charming took the diamond and carefully slid it into the hole. The hilt lit up as it secured the diamond.

"This isn't the magic of love or anything like that, is it?" Charming asked, suddenly suspicious.

"No." I stood up on shaky feet. "The magic of friendship trumps evil every time."

He grinned. "Is my sword magic now?"

"I think so." There was too much magic in the air for it not to be.

"Awesome."

"Now we have to fight the witch."

Charming kept his gaze on his glowing sword. "Fight the witch . . ." His dreamy smile faded. "Who is your grandmother. I finally get a magic sword and all I have to fight is someone's grandmother."

"She's not the best grandmother. Birthday presents from Grandma Perilous are the worst. They come via werewolf and are usually something terrible like a cockroach. I would rather get pajamas a half century out of style or a book I'll never read, like what most grandmothers give."

Charming's shoulders slumped. "I'm not sure if it's honorable to fight a grandmother."

"She's also an evil witch." I shuddered to emphasize her horribleness. "She locked my mom in a tower for seven years. She made Mr. Right go left, and who knows what happened to Mom's knight in shining armor. You were the only one left, and she destroyed your entire childhood."

"My childhood was spent learning to fight with a sword. I wouldn't call it ruined." He sheathed his sword. His weird scabbard, the one he'd made out of my hair, brightened and solidified, becoming something that resembled leather. More weird magic. "Come on. Let's find Amy and Edgar." He snickered. "Their names sound so cute together."

"They secretly like each other," I said. "That's why they hate each other so much." We scanned the meadow, but there wasn't any sign of Amy. Moonlight flooded the meadow as we picked our way toward the tower.

The ground rumbled, and a large vine shot up in front of us, which is never a good thing. We sidestepped the vine, and another one popped up.

"Magic vines!" Edgar yelled from the tower.

"We noticed!" I yelled back.

A long vine snaked toward me and wrapped around my ankle. Sharp thorns pierced my skin, and I screamed in pain. A look of sheer joy crossed Charming's face. He unsheathed his sword and slashed at the vicious vines.

"This is what I'm talking about!" Charming hacked at more vines while I peeled the dead one off my ankle. As quickly as he slashed through, more grew in. There was no way he could keep up with it, but I didn't have the heart to tell him so.

"Heads up!" Edgar yelled.

Flames shot from the tower and engulfed the vines. Charming and I ducked out of the way of the scorching heat.

"He's on our side, right?" Charming asked.

"It's always hard to tell with Edgar."

The flames died down, but the vines were still there. They weren't even singed. The vines bubbled and erupted in giant red flower buds.

"Not good," Charming said.

The buds closest to us turned in our direction and shot

fireballs at us. We ran the other way, but the vines had us surrounded.

"I thought your grandma wanted you alive." Charming ducked a fireball.

I was too busy dodging another fireball to answer. "Behind you!"

Charming pivoted but didn't have time to avoid the flames, so he did the only thing he could do. He swung his sword like a baseball bat and hit the fireball back at the vines. One of the buds leaned over and swallowed it whole.

I stood with my back to Charming's back. "Another one to the left—I mean, your right!" Charming managed to hit it with the flat of his blade. The fireball fell to the ground. I stomped out the fire with my amazing elf-made shoes. I didn't think they could be any more awesome than when I used them to climb, but I was wrong. They were fireproof too.

An opening appeared in the vines, and Edgar peered at us. "I can't keep this open all day. Are you two coming through?"

Charming and I dove through the opening.

"How did you get out of the tower?" I asked.

"I took the stairs." How nice for him.

Grandma Perilous appeared before us in a puff of black smoke. There was no sign of Amy. I hoped she'd escaped. "Eric Charming, you have been an annoyance since you first showed up. Fortunately, your curse is broken, so I can kill you now." Edgar and I moved in front of Charming. "I'll deal with you two later."

"No, Grandma Perilous," Edgar said. "You'll have to deal with us now." Edgar held his hands in front of him, flames ready.

"Charming is my friend," I said. "We stand with him."
A ruby fell from my lips.

Grandma Perilous laughed. "What are you going to do,
Raven? Throw jewels at me?"

Suddenly I felt totally useless. I didn't have a sword,
and I wasn't trained to use one anyway. Magic was not my
talent either. All I could do was look good.

Then I saw the jewel sparkling in Charming's hilt. I
helped make the sword magical after he'd already given up.
The carabiner dug into my skin, reminding me that I'd also
climbed up the side of a cliff.

"Sure, why not?" I said to Grandma Perilous. I grabbed
the ruby and threw it at her. It hit her in the chest, knocking her backward. "Do you have any idea what climbing
does for throwing arms?"

"First I'll put these boys in their place, and then I'll deal
with you, my dear. You don't need arms to make jewels. All
I need from you is tears."

I suddenly found myself in the tower. My trusty carabiner was gone, replaced with the horrible gold chains.
They came off easily since they were still broken. Below
me, Charming was trying to get at Grandma Perilous with
his sword, and Edgar was waving his hands around like a
lunatic. I could only assume that he was blocking or throwing spells.

I stepped over the broken chains and searched the room
for the stairs Edgar had used. The place looked terrible. I
couldn't imagine my poor mom living here for so long. I
peeked under the bed, but all I could find were a few loose
diamonds and a large gold chain link. I squeezed the link
in frustration, but it didn't bend. It was strong gold, probably reinforced with magic. I looped it over the bedpost.

There was nothing else in the room but the old bed and dust. I coughed. Lots and lots of dust. It was even all over the floor, except for a small area by the interior wall. I knelt and inspected the floor. The dust had been scraped back. That had to be a door. I'd just found the stairs.

I ran my fingers along the wall and found a tiny crack. Edgar had already opened it with magic. All I had to do was pull it open, but it was stuck. I pulled and pushed until my fingers were raw. Charming once told me that the evil witch used the stairs. Apparently, I wasn't evil enough for that.

A single diamond tear slipped down my cheek before flying across the room to the gold chains. Battle sounds floated up from the window. I checked to see how the boys were doing. Charming's sword flashed, and small sections of the meadow burned. It wasn't fair that the boys got to fight Grandma and I couldn't.

My diamond tear glinted in the moonlight. I knelt next to the pile of necklaces and saw that the diamond was attached to two different chains. The magic holding them together was strong. Mom did say that jewels were a princess's number one tool.

I dug all the stray diamonds out from under the bed and connected the necklaces together. When I ran out of diamonds, I sat down and said every kind word I knew. It was horrible, but it worked. The last chain connected with the golden link I'd put on the bedpost. I threw one end of the necklace out the window and climbed down the tower to the battle.

The boys had backed Grandma Perilous up against the tower wall. Her wand was at Edgar's feet. Edgar's hands were poised to throw another fireball.

"I missed the whole battle, didn't I?" I sighed. It was so unfair.

Charming looked at me and then up at the window. "Is that a giant necklace?" He ran his finger protectively over his blade.

Grandma Perilous didn't look nearly as angry or upset as I thought she should be. In fact, she looked downright smug.

Charming started back toward the forest. "Come on, Raven. Edgar's arms are going to get tired. We have to find someone to help us."

As soon as Charming's back was turned, Grandma Perilous twitched her fingers. Her wand flew into her hand.

"Charming!" I yelled. "Behind you!"

Charming spun around with his sword and swung. I couldn't see the spell, but I could hear it clink against his sword. Grandma Perilous suddenly didn't look so smug. She twitched her fingers to block the spell that Charming had reflected back at her. Light appeared in front of her whole body—except for the spot where my ruby had hit her before. Charming had reflected the spell perfectly. It hit her in the chest. Her eyes bulged, and she shrunk down until all that was left was a cockroach. Seeing her try to scurry away, Charming stuck a large rock on one of her legs. She struggled but couldn't move.

"Now you get to see how it feels to be a prisoner," I said to the squirming cockroach.

# Twenty-Four

A metallic clunking sound caught my attention. I turned to see Joe run out of the woods with Amy beside him. He still wore his armor, but he had the helmet tucked under his arm.

"Were you the one who was following us?" I asked Joe.

He nodded. "I've been following you since you escaped with the muffin man. I ran into a large thorny hedge just outside of the meadow and couldn't get to you."

"Why didn't you tell us you were there?"

"I wasn't sure if the witch was watching you. If she found out about me following, you wouldn't have had any backup. Turns out you didn't need me after all."

Amy locked me in a fierce hug. "I'm so glad you're okay!"

"I'm glad you're okay," I said.

"I'm okay," Edgar said, pointing to himself.

"You're okay," Charming said, pointing at Edgar.

"We're all okay," Charming and Edgar said together. They held their arms out to each other and then didn't hug. Boys.

"Joe is my grandfather," Amy said. "Years ago the witch came to our village and captured my parents. Grandpa took me in. He always talked about an uncle that I had never met. The same witch that took my parents was also responsible for his disappearance. When I found out that I had magical abilities, I thought I could sneak into the witch's hut to search for my family without her knowing. She caught me and forced me to be her servant. I never did find any of my family."

Joe picked the squirming cockroach off the ground and put it in a silver case. "I don't think I'll ever find my lost family, but at least the witch has been stopped. No one else will lose a loved one to her." He put his arm around Amy. "And I have my granddaughter back."

Ms. Darkwing appeared in the middle of our group. "Who's ready to go home?"

"I am so ready to go home," I said, raising my hand. A light breeze carrying the scent of stale gingerbread ruffled my hair. Grandma Perilous must have parked her old house somewhere nearby.

Edgar yawned and, in true boy style, didn't cover his open mouth. "Let's go."

Charming suddenly stopped grinning. "I'm not sure where home is anymore."

"Come with us to the real world," I said. "You can learn all you want about proper nutrition and junk." He could even have all of the healthy stuff my mom served me.

Ms. Darkwing put her hand on Charming's shoulder. "You have to have a designated adult to stay in the real world. My days of chasing after uprooted fairy-tale characters are over."

"I like the real world too." Amy sniffed. "The gingerbread house was never home, and the witch destroyed the village I grew up in."

"Then let's go to the real world," Joe said. "There isn't anything here for me anymore. My son is never coming back. You're all I have left."

"I could be Charming's designated adult," Ferran said, riding up on Betsy.

Ms. Darkwing laughed. "You two alone would be a recipe for disaster." She giggled. "I made a joke. Did you catch that? Recipe? Muffin man?"

Ferran cleared his throat. "That would have been true fourteen years ago, but not now. I grew up in a bakery. I have the skills I need to survive, but I never had a chance to have fun. Now is my chance to do what I want. Eric is like my brother."

Ms. Darkwing considered for a moment and then nodded. "I suppose we could try it."

Charming and Ferran high-fived. I couldn't help but grin. Life would have been terribly dull without Amy and Charming. And maybe I could talk Ferran into making something sweet every now and then.

Ms. Darkwing waved her wand, and Betsy turned into a small brown mouse. "That should help you get her into the real world. Just don't leave her in your pocket after midnight."

Branches crackled in the distance, and two figures broke through the tree line. Edgar and I exchanged looks. Mom had on a diamond necklace that sparkled brighter than Amy. Dad held a flame in his hand. They both looked around nervously, and I realized that Dad didn't rescue Mom. They escaped from Grandma Perilous together.

I ran across the clearing and put my arms around both my parents. I usually frown on public displays of affection, but I made an exception that time. Edgar squished in next to us.

"I used jewels to escape." I pointed to the diamond and gold chain glittering against the tower.

"I'm so glad," Mom said. "I would never have let you stay in that place for long."

"I was locked in there too," Edgar said. "But then I used the stairs."

We quickly introduced our parents to everyone. "Charming, Amy, Joe, and Ferran are all going to live in the real world with us," I told my parents.

"Ferran mentioned he might want to stay. I've already instructed our house to build new houses for them," Mom said.

"You instructed the house?" I didn't think anyone instructed our crazy house. I thought it just did whatever it wanted.

"Of course. It does have a mind of its own, but it also follows directions, mostly. I hoped that by having the house turn your room into a tower, you would see that you aren't powerless. The dungeon part was its idea."

Ms. Darkwing made a circle with her wand, and a glittery door appeared. We all stepped through and into the Forbidden Woods. Several trees had been shoved to the side, and a shiny new road cut into the woods. Two cozy cottages, complete with white trim, faced the side of my house.

"I didn't realize you were going to build us an entire house," Ferran said. "I thought you were just going to add a few rooms onto yours until we could find a place of our own."

"I thought about doing that, but I didn't want Raven

and Prince Charming living that close together." She gave me a look that might have been meaningful if I had any romantic feelings toward Charming. He was cute, but Happily Ever After was a long way away. "We had to build a new road to go into the woods," Mom continued. "We named the road Drury Lane so the muffin man would feel at home."

Ferran sighed.

A cockroach flew out of a tree and smacked Joe on the forehead. "Well, that's odd," Joe said, peeling the cockroach from his head.

"Sorry." Dad took the cockroach. "I can't imagine what's gotten into him."

I ducked behind Edgar before the roach got any ideas about flying into my hair again. "That's the cockroach Grandma Perilous sent to Edgar and me for our birthday."

"Your grandmother sent you a cockroach?" Joe scratched his chin. "I wonder . . . Ms. Darkwing, could you tell if this cockroach was enchanted?"

Ms. Darkwing nodded and waved her wand. The cockroach shimmered and vanished from Dad's hand. A young man appeared in front of Dad.

"James?" Joe said.

The young man turned to Joe. "Dad?" He ran and fell forward. "Where'd my other legs go?"

Joe brushed him off and engulfed him in a bear hug. "I thought I'd never see you again." Tears streamed down everyone's faces. Even I shed a tear or two, but they were regular tears now that we were back in the real world.

One of the houses rumbled, and another room popped out from the side.

"And I thought I had my hands full," Mom said. "What

are you going to do for a job, Joe? Ferran shouldn't have any problem setting up a bakery, but there isn't a demand for knights in shining armor around here. We'll help you where we can, but people get suspicious if I try to sell too many gems at once."

"We need a new gym teacher," Ms. Darkwing said. "Our last one ran away when he saw a giant lumberjack statue carry away one of his students. It's hard to get good help these days."

A knight in shining armor for a gym teacher? That should be interesting.

The others went to explore the new houses, but I stayed back with Mom. It had been a long day, and I was done exploring new places.

"So I'll have a knight in shining armor and Prince Charming living next door?" I asked. "Now all we need is to find Mr. Right."

"Mr. Right is here," Mom said. "He married a nice cheerleader, and they had a son. I can never remember his name, though."

"Kevin?" I asked.

Mom nodded. "That's the one. Do you know him?"

"We've met. They live down the street from us. Kevin gave me a ride home once. I guess he's Mr. Right too." But he needed a new car before anyone could take that title seriously. Even a horse was better than the pile of rust his mother drove around.

Mom suddenly looked uncomfortable and shifted her feet. "You're a little young to be looking for Mr. Right, aren't you?"

Of course I was, but she didn't have to know that I had no romantic interest in any of these boys . . . yet. "I don't have to look for Mr. Right, Mom. You just surrounded me with cute boys. Maybe I'll wear jewels to school now. Charming likes diamonds."

Her eyes widened, and she glanced at the new houses. "Um, maybe you could wait a few years before you wear jewels to school. This is the real world, after all."

There were definite advantages to having Prince Charming live next door.

I love my life.

# Discussion Questions

1.  Can you find some other literary references in the book?

2.  Why was Raven set on being evil?

3.  How many fairy tale elements can you find?

4.  Would you like to live in a house that was alive?

5.  Ms. Darkwing tells Raven and Charming that they both passed her test. Do you think the test was really about remembering Kevin's name? Why?

# About the Author

**J**anice Sperry lives in Utah with her husband, three children, and evil cat. She enjoys volunteering at the local elementary school and is exceptionally good at finding missing shoes, unless they are her own. Follow her blog at www.comeoutwhenyourehappy.blogspot.com.